Penguin Book C2795
The Speciality of the House and Other Stories

Stanley Ellin, who was born in New York City,
graduated from college in 1936, and has since been a
farmer, a teacher, and an iron worker. During the Second
World War he was in the U.S. Army.
His first story, *The Speciality of the House*, won an award
from the *Ellery Queen Mystery Magazine*, and further
stories won similar awards. These were published together in
this collection, which was selected in 1958 as one of the 100
most important books of the year and presented to the
White House Library.

His novels include *The Key to Nicholas Street*, *Dreadful
Summit* and *The Eighth Circle* (already published in
Penguins), and *The Winter After This Summer*. His latest
novel, *House of Cards*, was published in 1967. He is a three-
time winner of 'Edgar' Awards from the Mystery Writers of
America.

D1387328

St. John

with love from
Helen

August 1969

Stanley Ellin

The Specialty of the House and Other Stories

Penguin Books

Penguin Books Ltd, Harmondsworth,
Middlesex, England
Penguin Books Inc., 3300 Clipper Mill Road,
Baltimore, Md, 21211, U.S.A.
Penguin Books Australia Ltd, Ringwood,
Victoria, Australia

First published as Mystery Stories in the U.S.A. 1956
Published in Great Britain by
T. V. Boardman Ltd, 1957
Published in Penguin Books as The Specialty of
the House and other Stories, 1968
Copyright © Stanley Ellin, 1956

Made and printed in Great Britain by
Hunt Barnard & Co Ltd, Aylesbury, Bucks.
Set in Monotype Times Roman

To Janie

Contents

Foreword

Dear Reader:

It was on 22 November 1946, just one month after the closing of *EQMM*'s Second Annual Contest, that the Managing Editor of *Ellery Queen's Mystery Magazine* (at that time, Mildred Falk) telephoned us to discuss the day's editorial problems – yes, it was then, still is, and always will be 'problems'. She read aloud the more important letters in the day's mail and we suggested the tenor of the replies; she took corrections on the page proofs currently in work; she made notes, as we dictated, of the next month's ad (which always seems to have to go to press 'tonight'); she listed the titles we called off of books to be tracked down; yes, she would arrange for the translation of the new French story; together we untangled a knot in pagination; we exchanged opinions on the colour proof of the next issue's cover; no, she would not forget to send the cablegram ordering that rare first edition which turned up in London after five years of search. And so, the long voyage home each day, we arrived at the final question we always pop at our patient, long-suffering Managing Editor:

'Any new manuscripts in?'

'Yes, quite a batch.'

'Anything good?'

'A couple. They're being sent to you tonight.'

'Anything special?'

'Yes, there's one.'

'*Extra*-special?'

'Wait till you read it.'

'By anyone we know?'

'No. It came in direct, not through an agent. Might even be a "first story".'

Now, if there is anything we like better than a fine original by a 'name' author, it is a fine original by a newcomer. The thrill of discovery is still more exciting than that of rediscovery.

And so, back in November 1946, we were introduced to Stanley Ellin's first story, 'The Specialty of the House' (earliest title, 'The Kitchen at Robinson's'). Oh, frabjous day! Stanley was a young 30 at that time, married to a perfectly wonderful helpmate (Jeanne: 'a brilliant, remorseless and objective critic'), and their only child, Susan, was nearly six. (Your editors were an old 41 each.)

The history of 'The Specialty of the House' unfolded slowly in the beginning. With the author's approval we entered the story in *EQMM*'s Third Annual Contest, and a year later, at Christmastime 1947, it won a Special Prize – as the Best 'First Story' in the Third Contest. It was another four months before the story appeared in print – in the May 1948 issue of the *EQMM*. (By that time Stanley Ellin had written his first novel and Simon and Schuster had published it – DREADFUL SUMMIT, a fine book, brought out in April 1948.)

The good ship Stanley Ellin was launched. And from the day his first story made its debut, not a week seemed to pass that a friend or an acquaintance (and surprisingly often a complete stranger who had learned our identity) did not tap us from behind, resting a hand, almost tenderly, on our meaty shoulders; and when we turned around, we would invariably hear an awed comment on the lingering after-taste of Mr Ellin's shocker.

'So it was you,' they'd say, 'who published that story about lamb Amirstan. What a yarn! It was terrific. I still have goose pimples!'

We shuddered every time. The *frisson d'horreur* experienced by each person who accosted us was so genuine, so enduring. . . .

Later the same year the story was included in THE QUEEN'S AWARDS, 1948, and hardly a month seems to pass – for nearly a decade now – that someone doesn't stop us in the street, or corner us at a meeting, or interrupt us during a meal (that is always the worst – being tapped, almost tenderly, *while eating*!), and say: 'Why don't you publish more stories like that one about the restaurant – you know, that "Specialty of the House" story? That was a knockout!'

The readers never forget it. We never forgot it. The simple truth was that 'The Specialty of the House' proved to be an unforgettable story. By now it is almost a legendary story. And because it has become a modern classic in its field, it is perhaps time that we made a confession for the good of our souls. For it was Queen who awarded the story a Special Prize as the Best 'First Story' of its year; but there were many – readers and critics alike – who thought Queen guilty of a classic blunder. There were many who thought 'The Specialty of the House' deserved a higher prize – indeed, First Prize as the best story of that year's contest.

Anthony Boucher called it 'a subtle masterpiece' and 'the best first-published story I've ever read'. Other critics echoed that judgement. That extraordinarily perceptive devotee of crime and cauld grue, Christopher Morley, wrote in the *Book-of-the-Month News* that 'The Specialty of the House' was 'worth all the rest of THE QUEEN'S AWARDS, 1948 together ... for macaber and skill in suspense it is worth a double-jaw of porcelain false teeth ... for the connoisseur it is the *echt Blutwurst* and gravy.'

After that, Stanley Ellin wrote a story for each succeeding Annual Contest conducted by *Ellery Queen's Mystery Magazine* – and his record is phenomenal. He won a Third Prize in our Fourth Contest. He won successive Second Prizes in our Fifth and Sixth Contests. (In April 1952 Simon and Schuster published Stanley Ellin's second novel, THE KEY TO NICHOLAS STREET, an even finer book than his first novel.) In our Seventh and Eighth Contests he again won Second Prizes. In our Ninth Contest he made it five Second Prizes in a row – for 'The House Party' – and in April 1955 Stanley Ellin received (for 'The House Party' and the general excellence of all his short stories) the coveted Edgar awarded annually by the Mystery Writers of America; on the night of the award Susan was 14 and quite a young lady – and how proud she was of her dad! Then, in our Tenth Contest, whose winners were announced at the end of 1954, Stanley Ellin's 'The Moment of Decision' won First Prize – the highest award *EQMM* can give to any writer in any year.

And during that near-decade Mr Ellin's talent grew and matured and became a thing of beauty. From the very beginning, back in 1946, he had solidity and substance – solidity and texture in his style, substance and imagination in his plots. But with the years, with his unflagging zest, his almost incredible conscientiousness, his hypersensitivity to the impact of horror which lurks not only in the 'specialties' of life but equally, perhaps even more shockingly, in the 'orderly world' about us – with and through all these Stanley Ellin's stature as a writer grew and his work flashed new tones; for undeniably there are bigger meanings in his later stories, larger problems delved into, subtler nuances revealed in his characters and in the events that lead up to – and inevitably follow – the tragedies of modern living.

We have Mr Ellin's own words for his methods, for his trials and tribulations as that mysterious organism called 'the professional writer'. We know, for example, that his dream of an ideal workroom is 'Proust's cork-lined chamber plus a typewriter'. We know (from his contributions to THE MYSTERY WRITERS' HANDBOOK, a 'tec textbook by the Mystery Writers of America, edited by Herbert Brean, Harper's, 1956) that his biggest stumbling block is 'writing the first paragraph'. He writes page after page of single opening paragraphs until he 'hits one that *feels* right'. But it is both a startling and an impressive fact that he has discarded as many as forty-two opening paragraphs before being reasonably satisfied to go on to paragraph two. His themes are not tricky or artificial – you won't find 'gimmicks' in Mr Ellin's stories. Usually he starts with what he calls 'a sociological concept: the tragedy of the civil-service mentality which sells everything for economic security; the effects of a murder on an apparently rock-ribbed middle-class family; the veering of American youth to mink-coat-and-Cadillac standards.'

He writes sporadically. Each working day he walks miles, reads every newspaper published in New York City, all the time 'stewing' over the embryo of a story idea. Then, when the embryo has developed to full growth, he locks himself in his working room and writes eight to fourteen uninterrupted hours a day until the job is done. Each page is rewritten as it is completed, before he proceeds to the next. Sometimes each page is rewritten only once (a miracle), more often five or six times, and occasionally (and in this, Mr Ellin admits, 'lies madness') a dozen or more times. But that is the Ellin method: he cannot move on to the next page until the previous one is as polished and gleaming as its creator can make it. As a result, Mr Ellin's writing pace is comparatively slow, and it is made even slower by the unavoidable circumstance that he usually stews and mulls and meditates for weeks and weeks on a plot kernel before he finally gets to writing that first first-paragraph.

About the man himself, his background, what he looks like? Well, he was born 6 October 1916, in New York City. His education includes a B.A. from Brooklyn College in 1936 and professional status as a boilermaker's apprentice. Before he began to write full time, he was a steelworker. His favourite recreations are watching football, boxing, and ballet, listening to opera and good conversation – and baseball. What a Brooklyn Dodger fan he is! And how he 'hates' the New York Giants! He is of average height but otherwise big and stocky. He likes to compare his looks with that of an 'Alaskan brown bear who has been preparing himself for a hard winter'. Close up, he gives (in his own words) 'the curiously unfinished appearance of an Epstein sculpture'. He is definitely not a man easily lost in a crowd, and we don't know a single person who does not like, respect, and admire him ...

And now we have Stanley Ellin's first book of short stories. It contains ten tales, arranged in chronological order of their writing, beginning with that classic first, 'The Specialty of the House', and ending with his First Prize story of 1955, 'The Moment of Decision'. We are proud to have discovered Stanley Ellin (an admittedly boastful and conceited way of expressing our small part in his accomplishments); we are proud that every short story of crime, detection, and mystery that Mr Ellin has written has appeared first in *Ellery Queen's Mystery Magazine*; and we are proud to have been asked to write a foreword to Mr Ellin's first volume of short stories.

And there is one thing more we would like to say: In our opinion, Mr Ellin's book of short stories is an important book in its genre, and we want to stamp its importance as indelibly as we can. So here and now, we nominate MYSTERY STORIES by Stanley Ellin to Queen's Quorum, which is the continuing record of the most important books of detective-crime-mystery short stories ever published, beginning 111 years ago with Edgar A. Poe's TALES.

Stanley Ellin's MYSTERY STORIES stands shoulder to meaty shoulder with the great modern books in its field. It is Queen's Quorum Number 113 – and long may it remain in print.

ELLERY QUEEN

The Specialty of the House

'And this,' said Laffler, 'is Sbirro's.' Costain saw a square brown-stone façade identical with the others that extended from either side into the clammy darkness of the deserted street. From the barred windows of the basement at his feet, a glimmer of light showed behind heavy curtains.

'Lord,' he observed, 'it's a dismal hole, isn't it?'

'I beg you to understand,' said Laffler stiffly, 'that Sbirro's is the restaurant without pretensions. Besieged by these ghastly, neurotic times, it has refused to compromise. It is perhaps the last important establishment in this city lit by gas jets. Here you will find the same honest furnishings, the same magnificent Sheffield service, and possibly, in a far corner, the very same spider webs that were remarked by the patrons of a half century ago!'

'A doubtful recommendation,' said Costain, 'and hardly sanitary.'

'When you enter,' Laffler continued, 'you leave the insanity of this year, this day, and this hour, and you find yourself for a brief span restored in spirit, not by opulence, but by dignity, which is the lost quality of our time.'

Costain laughed uncomfortably. 'You make it sound more like a cathedral than a restaurant,' he said.

In the pale reflection of the street lamp overhead, Laffler peered at his companion's face. 'I wonder,' he said abruptly, 'whether I have not made a mistake in extending this invitation to you.'

Costain was hurt. Despite an impressive title and large salary, he was no more than clerk to this pompous little man, but he was impelled to make some display of his feelings. 'If you wish,' he said coldly, 'I can make other plans for my evening with no trouble.'

With his large, cowlike eyes turned up to Costain, the mist

drifting into the ruddy, full moon of his face, Laffler seemed strangely ill at ease. Then 'No, no,' he said at last, 'absolutely not. It's important that you dine at Sbirro's with me.' He grasped Costain's arm firmly and led the way to the wrought-iron gate of the basement. 'You see, you're the sole person in my office who seems to know anything at all about good food. And on my part, knowing about Sbirro's but not having some appreciative friend to share it is like having a unique piece of art locked in a room where no one else can enjoy it.'

Costain was considerably mollified by this. 'I understand there are a great many people who relish that situation.'

'I'm not one of that kind!' Laffler said sharply. 'And having the secret of Sbirro's locked in myself for years has finally become unendurable.' He fumbled at the side of the gate and from within could be heard the small, discordant jangle of an ancient pull-bell. An interior door opened with a groan, and Costain found himself peering into a dark face whose only discernible feature was a row of gleaming teeth.

'Sair?' said the face.

'Mr Laffler and a guest.'

'Sair,' the face said again, this time in what was clearly an invitation. It moved aside and Costain stumbled down a single step behind his host. The door and gate creaked behind him, and he stood blinking in a small foyer. It took him a moment to realize that the figure he now stared at was his own reflection in a gigantic pier glass that extended from floor to ceiling. 'Atmosphere', he said under his breath and chuckled as he followed his guide to a seat.

He faced Laffler across a small table for two and peered curiously around the dining-room. It was no size at all, but the half-dozen guttering gas jets which provided the only illumination threw such a deceptive light that the walls flickered and faded into uncertain distance.

There were no more than eight or ten tables about, arranged to insure the maximum privacy. All were occupied, and the few waiters serving them moved with quiet efficiency. In the air were a soft clash and scrape of cutlery and a soothing murmur of talk. Costain nodded appreciatively.

Laffler breathed an audible sigh of gratification. 'I knew you would share my enthusiasm,' he said. 'Have you noticed, by the way, that there are no women present?'

Costain raised inquiring eyebrows.

'Sbirro,' said Laffler, 'does not encourage members of the fair sex to enter the premises. And, I can tell you, his method is decidedly effective. I had the experience of seeing a woman get a taste of it not long ago. She sat at a table for not less than an hour waiting for service which was never forthcoming.'

'Didn't she make a scene?'

'She did.' Laffler smiled at the recollection. 'She succeeded in annoying the customers, embarrassing her partner, and nothing more.'

'And what about Mr Sbirro?'

'He did not make an appearance. Whether he directed affairs from behind the scenes, or was not even present during the episode, I don't know. Whichever it was, he won a complete victory. The woman never reappeared nor, for that matter, did the witless gentleman who by bringing her was really the cause of the entire contretemps.'

'A fair warning to all present,' laughed Costain.

A waiter now appeared at the table. The chocolate-dark skin, the thin, beautifully moulded nose and lips, the large liquid eyes, heavily lashed, and the silver white hair so heavy and silken that it lay on the skull like a cap, all marked him definitely as an East Indian of some sort, Costain decided. The man arranged the stiff table linen, filled two tumblers from a huge, cut-glass pitcher, and set them in their proper places.

'Tell me,' Laffler said eagerly, 'is the special being served this evening?'

The waiter smiled regretfully and showed teeth as spectacular as those of the major domo. 'I am so sorry, sair. There is no special this evening.'

Laffler's face fell into lines of heavy disappointment. 'After waiting so long. It's been a month already, and I hoped to show my friend here ...'

'You understand the difficulties, sair.'

'Of course, of course.' Laffler looked at Costain sadly and

shrugged. 'You see, I had in mind to introduce you to the greatest treat that Sbirro's offers, but unfortunately it isn't on the menu this evening.'

The waiter said, 'Do you wish to be served now, sair?' and Laffler nodded. To Costain's surprise the waiter made his way off without waiting for any instructions.

'Have you ordered in advance?' he asked.

'Ah,' said Laffler, 'I really should have explained. Sbirro's offers no choice whatsoever. You will eat the same meal as everyone else in this room. Tomorrow evening you would eat an entirely different meal, but again without designating a single preference.'

'Very unusual,' said Costain, 'and certainly unsatisfactory at times. What if one doesn't have a taste for the particular dish set before him?'

'On that score,' said Laffler solemnly, 'you need have no fears. I give you my word that no matter how exciting your tastes, you will relish every mouthful you eat in Sbirro's.'

Costain looked doubtful, and Laffler smiled. 'And consider the subtle advantages of the system,' he said. 'When you pick up the menu of a popular restaurant, you find yourself confronted with innumerable choices. You are forced to weigh, to evaluate, to make uneasy decisions which you may instantly regret. The effect of all this is a tension which, however slight, must make for discomfort.

'And consider the mechanics of the process. Instead of a hurly-burly of sweating cooks rushing about a kitchen in a frenzy to prepare a hundred varying items, we have a chef who stands serenely alone, bringing all his talents to bear on one task, with all assurance of a complete triumph!'

'Then you have seen the kitchen?'

'Unfortunately, no,' said Laffler sadly. 'The picture I offer is hypothetical, made of conversational fragments I have pieced together over the years. I must admit, though, that my desire to see the functioning of the kitchen here comes very close to being my sole obsession nowadays.'

'But have you mentioned this to Sbirro?'

'A dozen times. He shrugs the suggestion away.'

'Isn't that a rather curious foible on his part?'

'No, no,' Laffler said hastily, 'a master artist is never under the compulsion of petty courtesies. Still,' he sighed, 'I have never given up hope.'

The waiter now reappeared bearing two soup bowls which he set in place with mathematical exactitude, and a small tureen from which he slowly ladled a measure of clear, thin broth. Costain dipped his spoon into the broth and tasted it with some curiosity. It was delicately flavoured, bland to the verge of taste-lessness. Costain frowned, tentatively reached for the salt and pepper cellars, and discovered there were none on the table. He looked up, saw Laffler's eyes on him, and although unwilling to compromise with his own tastes, he hesitated to act as a damper on Laffler's enthusiasm. Therefore he smiled and indicated the broth.

'Excellent,' he said.

Laffler returned his smile. 'You do not find it excellent at all,' he said coolly. 'You find it flat and badly in need of condiments. I know this,' he continued as Costain's eyebrows shot upward, 'because it was my own reaction many years ago, and because like yourself I found myself reaching for salt and pepper after the first mouthful. I also learned with surprise that condiments are not available in Sbirro's.'

Costain was shocked. 'Not even salt!' he exclaimed.

'Not even salt. The very fact that you require it for your soup stands as evidence that your taste is unduly jaded. I am confident that you will now make the same discovery that I did: by the time you have nearly finished your soup, your desire for salt will be nonexistent.'

Laffler was right; before Costain had reached the bottom of his plate, he was relishing the nuances of the broth with steadily in-creasing delight. Laffler thrust aside his own empty bowl and rested his elbows on the table. 'Do you agree with me now?'

'To my surprise,' said Costain, 'I do.'

As the waiter busied himself clearing the table, Laffler lowered his voice significantly. 'You will find,' he said, 'that the absence of condiments is but one of several noteworthy characteristics which mark Sbirro's. I may as well prepare you for these. For example, no alcoholic beverages of any sort are served here, nor for that matter any beverage except clear, cold water, the first and only drink necessary for a human being.'

'Outside of mother's milk,' suggested Costain dryly.

'I can answer that in like vein by pointing out that the average patron of Sbirro's has passed that primal stage of his development.'

Costain laughed. 'Granted,' he said.

'Very well. There is also a ban on the use of tobacco in any form.'

'But good heavens,' said Costain, 'doesn't that make Sbirro's more a teetotaller's retreat than a gourmet's sanctuary?'

'I fear,' said Laffler solemnly, 'that you confuse the words, *gourmet* and *gourmand*. The gourmand, through glutting himself, requires a wider and wider latitude of experience to stir his surfeited senses, but the very nature of the gourmet is simplicity. The ancient Greek in his coarse chiton savouring the ripe olive; the Japanese in his bare room contemplating the curve of a single flower stem – these are the true gourmets.'

'But an occasional drop of brandy or pipeful of tobacco,' said Costain dubiously, 'are hardly over-indulgences.'

'By alternating stimulant and narcotic,' said Laffler, 'you see-saw the delicate balance of your taste so violently that it loses its most precious quality: the appreciation of fine food. During my years as a patron of Sbirro's, I have proved this to my satisfaction.'

'May I ask,' said Costain, 'why you regard the ban on these things as having such deep aesthetic motives? What about such mundane reasons as the high cost of a liquor licence, or the possibility that patrons would object to the smell of tobacco in such confined quarters?'

Laffler shook his head violently. 'If and when you meet Sbirro,' he said, 'you will understand at once that he is not the man to make decisions on a mundane basis. As a matter of fact, it was Sbirro himself who first made me cognizant of what you call "aesthetic" motives.'

'An amazing man,' said Costain as the waiter prepared to serve the entrée.

Laffler's next words were not spoken until he had savoured and swallowed a large portion of meat. 'I hesitate to use superlatives,' he said, 'but to my way of thinking, Sbirro represents man at the apex of his civilization!'

Costain cocked an eyebrow and applied himself to his roast which rested in a pool of stiff gravy ungarnished by green or vegetable. The thin steam rising from it carried to his nostrils a subtle, tantalizing odour which made his mouth water. He chewed a piece as slowly and thoughtfully as if he were analysing the intricacies of a Mozart symphony. The range of taste he discovered was really extraordinary, from the pungent nip of the crisp outer edge to the peculiarly flat yet soul-satisfying ooze of blood which the pressure of his jaws forced from the half-raw interior.

Upon swallowing he found himself ferociously hungry for another piece, and then another, and it was only with an effort that he prevented himself from wolfing down all his share of the meat and gravy without waiting to get the full voluptuous satisfaction from each mouthful. When he had scraped his platter clean, he realized that both he and Laffler had completed the entire course without exchanging a single word. He commented on this, and Laffler said: 'Can you see any need for words in the presence of such food?'

Costain looked around at the shabby, dimly lit room, the quiet diners, with a new perception. 'No,' he said humbly, 'I cannot. For any doubts I had I apologize unreservedly. In all your praise of Sbirro's there was not a single word of exaggeration.'

'Ah,' said Laffler delightedly. 'And that is only part of the story. You heard me mention the special which unfortunately was not on the menu tonight. What you have just eaten is as nothing when compared to the absolute delights of that special!'

'Good Lord!' cried Costain. 'What is it? Nightingales' tongues? Filet of unicorn?'

'Neither,' said Laffler. 'It is lamb.'

'Lamb?'

Laffler remained lost in thought for a minute. 'If,' he said at last, 'I were to give you in my own unstinted words my opinion of this dish, you would judge me completely insane. That is how deeply the mere thought of it affects me. It is neither the fatty chop, nor the too solid leg; it is, instead, a select portion of the rarest sheep in existence and is named after the species – lamb Amirstan.'

Costain knit his brows. 'Amirstan?'

'A fragment of desolation almost lost on the border which separates Afghanistan and Russia. From chance remarks dropped by Sbirro, I gather it is no more than a plateau which grazes the pitiful remnants of a flock of superb sheep. Sbirro, through some means or other, obtained rights to the traffic in this flock, and is, therefore, the sole restaurateur ever to have lamb Amirstan on his bill of fare. I can tell you that the appearance of this dish is a rare occurrence indeed, and luck is the only guide in determining for the clientele the exact date when it will be served.'

'But sure,' said Costain, 'Sbirro could provide some advance knowledge of this event.'

'The objection to that is simply stated,' said Laffler. 'There exists in this city a huge number of professional gluttons. Should advance information slip out, it is quite likely that they will, out of curiosity, become familiar with the dish and thenceforth supplant the regular patrons at these tables.'

'But you don't mean to say,' objected Costain, 'that these few people present are the only ones in the entire city, or for that matter, in the whole wide world, who know of the existence of Sbirro's!'

'Very nearly. There may be one or two regular patrons who, for some reason, are not present at the moment.'

'That's incredible.'

'It is done,' said Laffler, the slightest shade of menace in his voice, 'by every patron making it his solemn obligation to keep the secret. By accepting my invitation this evening, you automatically assume that obligation. I hope you can be trusted with it.'

Costain flushed. 'My position in your employ should vouch for me. I only question the wisdom of a policy which keeps such magnificent food away from so many who would enjoy it.'

'Do you know the inevitable result of the policy *you* favour?' asked Laffler bitterly. 'An influx of idiots who would nightly complain that they are never served roast duck with chocolate sauce. Is that picture tolerable to you?'

'No,' admitted Costain, 'I am forced to agree with you.'

Laffler leaned back in his chair wearily and passed his hand over his eyes in an uncertain gesture. 'I am a solitary man,' he said quietly, 'and not by choice alone. It may sound strange to you, it may border on eccentricity, but I feel to my depths that this restaurant, this warm haven in a coldly insane world, is both family and friend to me.'

And Costain, who to this moment had never viewed his companion as other than tyrannical employer or officious host, now felt an overwhelming pity twist inside his comfortably expanded stomach.

By the end of two weeks the invitations to join Laffler at Sbirro's had become something of a ritual. Every day, at a few minutes after five, Costain would step out into the office corridor and lock his cubicle behind him; he would drape his overcoat neatly over his left arm, and peer into the glass of the door to make sure his Homburg was set at the proper angle. At one time he would have followed this by lighting a cigarette, but under Laffler's prodding he had decided to give abstinence a fair trial. Then he would start down the corridor, and Laffler would fall in step at his elbow, clearing his throat. 'Ah, Costain. No plans for this evening, I hope.'

'No,' Costain would say, 'I'm footloose and fancy-free,' or 'At your service,' or something equally inane. He wondered at times whether it would not be more tactful to vary the ritual with an occasional refusal, but the glow with which Laffler received his answer, and the rough friendliness of Laffler's grip on his arm, forestalled him.

Among the treacherous crags of the business world, reflected Costain, what better way to secure your footing than friendship with one's employer. Already, a secretary close to the workings of the inner office had commented publicly on Laffler's highly favourable opinion of Costain. That was all to the good.

And the food! The incomparable food at Sbirro's! For the first time in his life, Costain, ordinarily a lean and bony man, noted with gratification that he was certainly gaining weight; within two weeks his bones had disappeared under a layer of sleek, firm flesh, and here and there were even signs of incipient plumpness. It struck Costain one night, while surveying himself in his bath, that the rotund Laffler, himself, might have been a spare and bony man before discovering Sbirro's.

So there was obviously everything to be gained and nothing to be lost by accepting Laffler's invitations. Perhaps after testing the heralded wonders of lamb Amirstan and meeting Sbirro, who thus far had not made an appearance, a refusal or two might be in order. But certainly not until then.

That evening, two weeks to a day after his first visit to Sbirro's, Costain had both desires fulfilled: he dined on lamb Amirstan, and he met Sbirro. Both exceeded all his expectations.

When the waiter leaned over their table immediately after seating them and gravely announced: 'Tonight is special, sair,' Costain was shocked to find his heart pounding with expectation. On the table before him he saw Laffler's hands trembling violently. But it isn't natural, he thought suddenly. Two full grown men, presumably intelligent and in the full possession of their senses, as jumpy as a pair of cats waiting to have their meat flung to them!

'This is it!' Laffler's voice startled him so that he almost leaped from his seat. 'The culinary triumph of all times! And faced by it you are embarrassed by the very emotions it distils.'

'How did you know that?' Costain asked faintly.

'How? Because a decade ago I underwent your embarrassment. Add to that your air of revulsion and it's easy to see how affronted you are by the knowledge that man has not yet forgotten how to slaver over his meat.'

'And these others,' whispered Costain, 'do they all feel the same thing?'

'Judge for yourself.'

Costain looked furtively around at the nearby tables. 'You are right,' he finally said. 'At any rate, there's comfort in numbers.'

Laffler inclined his head slightly to the side. 'One of the numbers,' he remarked, 'appears to be in for a disappointment.'

Costain followed the gesture. At the table indicated a grey-haired man sat conspicuously alone, and Costain frowned at the empty chair opposite him.

'Why, yes,' he recalled, 'that very stout, bald man, isn't it? I believe it's the first dinner he's missed here in two weeks.'

'The entire decade more likely,' said Laffler sympathetically. 'Rain or shine, crisis or calamity. I don't think he's missed an evening at Sbirro's since the first time I dined here. Imagine his expression when he's told that, on his very first defection, lamb Amirstan was the *plat du jour*.'

Costain looked at the empty chair again with a dim discomfort. 'His very first?' he murmured.

'Mr Laffler! And friend! I am so pleased. So very, very pleased. No, do not stand; I will have a place made.' Miraculously a seat appeared under the figure standing there at the table. 'The lamb Amirstan will be an unqualified success, hurr? I myself have been stewing in the miserable kitchen all the day, prodding the foolish chef to do everything just so. The just so is the important part, hurr? But I see your friend does not know me. An introduction, perhaps?'

The words ran in a smooth, fluid eddy. They rippled, they purred, they hypnotized Costain so that he could do no more than stare. The mouth that uncoiled this sinuous monologue was alarmingly wide, with thin mobile lips that curled and twisted with every syllable. There was a flat nose with a straggling line of hair under it; wide-set eyes, almost oriental in appearance, that glittered in the unsteady flare of gaslight: and long, sleek hair that swept back from high on the unwrinkled forehead – hair so pale that it might have been bleached of all colour. An amazing face surely, and the sight of it tortured Costain with the conviction that it was somehow familiar. His brain twitched and prodded but could not stir up any solid recollection.

Laffler's voice jerked Costain out of his study. 'Mr Sbirro. Mr Costain, a good friend and associate.' Costain rose and shook the proferred hand. It was warm and dry, flint-hard against his palm.

'I am so very pleased, Mr Costain. So very, very pleased,' purred the voice. 'You like my little establishment, hurr? You have a great treat in store, I assure you.'

Laffler chuckled. 'Oh, Costain's been dining here regularly for two weeks,' he said. 'He's by way of becoming a great admirer of yours, Sbirro.'

The eyes were turned on Costain. 'A very great compliment.

You compliment me with your presence and I return same with my food, hurr? But the lamb Amirstan is far superior to anything of your past experience, I assure you. All the trouble of obtaining it, all the difficulty of preparation, is truly merited.'

Costain strove to put aside the exasperating problem of that face. 'I have wondered,' he said, 'why with all these difficulties you mention, you even bother to present lamb Amirstan to the public. Surely your other dishes are excellent enough to uphold your reputation.'

Sbirro smiled so broadly that his face became perfectly round. 'Perhaps it is a matter of the psychology, hurr? Someone discovers a wonder and must share it with others. He must fill his cup to the brim, perhaps, by observing the so evident pleasure of those who explore it with him. Or,' he shrugged, 'perhaps it is just a matter of good business.'

'Then in the light of all this,' Costain persisted, 'and considering all the conventions you have imposed on your customers, why do you open the restaurant to the public instead of operating it as a private club?'

The eyes abruptly glinted into Costain's, then turned away. 'So perspicacious, hurr? Then I will tell you. Because there is more privacy in a public eating place than in the most exclusive club in existence! Here no one inquires of your affairs; no one desires to know the intimacies of your life. Here the business is eating. We are not curious about names and addresses or the reasons for the coming and going of our guests. We welcome you when you are here; we have no regrets when you are here no longer. That is the answer, hurr?'

Costain was startled by this vehemence. 'I had no intention of prying,' he stammered.

Sbirro ran the tip of his tongue over his thin lips. 'No, no,' he reassured, 'you are not prying. Do not let me give you that impression. On the contrary, I invite your questions.'

'Oh, come, Costain,' said Laffler. 'Don't let Sbirro intimidate you. I've known him for years and I guarantee that his bark is worse than his bite. Before you know it, he'll be showing you all the privileges of the house – outside of inviting you to visit his precious kitchen, of course.'

'Ah,' smiled Sbirro, 'for that, Mr Costain may have to wait a little while. For everything else I am at his beck and call.'

Laffler slapped his hand jovially on the table. 'What did I tell you!' he said. 'Now let's have the truth, Sbirro. Has anyone, outside of your staff, ever stepped into the sanctum sanctorum?'

Sbirro looked up. 'You see on the wall above you,' he said earnestly, 'the portrait of one to whom I did the honour. A very dear friend and a patron of most long standing, he is evidence that my kitchen is not inviolate.'

Costain studied the picture and started with recognition. 'Why,' he said excitedly, 'that's the famous writer – you know the one, Laffler – he used to do such wonderful short stories and cynical bits and then suddenly took himself off and disappeared in Mexico!'

'Of course!' cried Laffler, 'and to think I've been sitting under his portrait for years without even realizing it?' He turned to Sbirro. 'A dear friend, you say? His disappearance must have been a blow to you.'

Sbirro's face lengthened. 'It was, it was, I assure you. But think of it this way, gentlemen: he was probably greater in his death than in his life, hurr? A most tragic man, he often told me that his only happy hours were spent here at this very table. Pathetic, is it not? And to think the only favour I could ever show him was to let him witness the mysteries of my kitchen, which is, when all is said and done, no more than a plain, ordinary kitchen.'

'You seem very certain of his death,' commented Costain. 'After all, no evidence has ever turned up to substantiate it.'

Sbirro contemplated the picture. 'None at all,' he said softly. 'Remarkable, hurr?'

With the arrival of the entrée Sbirro leaped to his feet and set about serving them himself. With his eyes alight he lifted the casserole from the tray and sniffed at the fragrance from within with sensual relish. Then, taking great care not to lose a single drop of gravy, he filled two platters with chunks of dripping meat. As if exhausted by this task, he sat back in his chair, breathing heavily. 'Gentlemen,' he said, 'to your good appetite.'

Costain chewed his first mouthful with great deliberation and swallowed it. Then he looked at the empty tines of his fork with glazed eyes.

'Good God!' he breathed.

'It is good, hurr? Better than you imagined?'

Costain shook his head dazedly. 'It is as impossible,' he said slowly, 'for the uninitiated to conceive the delights of lamb Amirstan as for mortal man to look into his own soul.'

'Perhaps – ' Sbirro thrust his head so close that Costain could feel the warm, fetid breath tickle his nostrils – 'perhaps you have just had a glimpse into your soul, hurr?'

Costain tried to draw back slightly without giving offence. 'Perhaps.' He laughed. 'And a gratifying picture it made: all fang and claw. But without intending any disrespect, I should hardly like to build my church on *lamb en casserole*.'

Sbirro rose and laid a hand gently on his shoulder. 'So perspicacious,' he said. 'Sometimes when you have nothing to do, nothing, perhaps, but sit for a very little while in a dark room and think of this world – what it is and what it is going to be – then you must turn your thoughts a little to the significance of the Lamb in religion. It will be so interesting. And now – ' he bowed deeply to both men – 'I have held you long enough from your dinner. I was most happy,' he said, nodding to Costain, 'and I am sure we will meet again.' The teeth gleamed, the eyes glittered, and Sbirro was gone down the aisle of tables.

Costain twisted around to stare after the retreating figure. 'Have I offended him in some way?' he asked.

Laffler looked up from his plate. 'Offended him? He loves that kind of talk. Lamb Amirstan is a ritual with him; get him started and he'll be back at you a dozen times worse than a priest making a conversion.'

Costain turned to his meal with the face still hovering before him. 'Interesting man,' he reflected. 'Very.'

It took him a month to discover the tantalizing familiarity of that face, and when he did, he laughed aloud in his bed. Why, of course! Sbirro might have sat as the model for the Cheshire cat in *Alice*!

He passed this thought on to Laffler the very next evening as they pushed their way down the street to the restaurant against a chill, blustering wind. Laffler only looked blank.

'You may be right,' he said, 'but I'm not a fit judge. It's a far cry back to the days when I read the book. A far cry, indeed.'

As if taking up his words, a piercing howl came ringing down the street and stopped both men short in their tracks. 'Someone's in trouble there,' said Laffler. 'Look!'

Not far from the entrance to Sbirro's two figures could be seen struggling in the near darkness. They swayed back and forth and suddenly tumbled into a writhing heap on the sidewalk. The piteous howl went up again, and Laffler, despite his girth, ran toward it at a fair speed with Costain tagging cautiously behind.

Stretched out full-length on the pavement was a slender figure with the dusky complexion and white hair of one of Sbirro's servitors. His fingers were futilely plucking at the huge hands which encircled his throat, and his knees pushed weakly up at the gigantic bulk of a man who brutally bore down with his full weight.

Laffler came up panting. 'Stop this!' he shouted. 'What's going on here?'

The pleading eyes almost bulging from their sockets turned toward Laffler. 'Help, sair. This man – drunk – '

'Drunk am I, ya dirty –' Costain saw now that the man was a sailor in a badly soiled uniform. The air around him reeked with the stench of liquor. 'Pick me pocket and then call me drunk, will ya!' He dug his fingers in harder, and his victim groaned.

Laffler seized the sailor's shoulder. 'Let go of him, do you hear! Let go of him at once!' he cried, and the next instant was sent careening into Costain, who staggered back under the force of the blow.

The attack on his own person sent Laffler into immediate and berserk action. Without a sound he leaped at the sailor, striking and kicking furiously at the unprotected face and flanks. Stunned at first, the man came to his feet with a rush and turned on Laffler. For a moment they stood locked together, and then as Costain joined the attack, all three went sprawling to the ground. Slowly Laffler and Costain got to their feet and looked down at the body before them.

'He's either out cold from liquor,' said Costain, 'or he struck his head going down. In any case, it's a job for the police.'

'No, no, sair!' The waiter crawled weakly to his feet, and stood swaying. 'No police, sair. Mr Sbirro do not want such. You understand, sair.' He caught hold of Costain with a pleading hand, and Costain looked at Laffler.

'Of course not,' said Laffler. 'We won't have to bother with the police. They'll pick him up soon enough, the murderous sot. But what in the world started all this?'

'That man, sair. He make most erratic way while walking, and with no meaning I push against him. Then he attack me, accusing me to rob him.'

'As I thought.' Laffler pushed the waiter gently along. 'Now go on in and get yourself attended to.'

The man seemed ready to burst into tears. 'To you, sair, I owe my life. If there is anything I can do – '

Laffler turned into the areaway that led to Sbirro's door. 'No, no, it was nothing. You go along, and if Sbirro has any questions send him to me. I'll straighten it out.'

'My life, sair,' were the last words they heard as the inner door closed behind them.

'There you are, Costain,' said Laffler, as a few minutes later he drew his chair under the table, 'civilized man in all his glory. Reeking with alcohol, strangling to death some miserable innocent who came too close.'

Costain made an effort to gloss over the nerve-shattering memory of the episode. 'It's the neurotic cat that takes to alcohol,' he said. 'Surely there's a reason for that sailor's condition.'

'Reason? Of course there is. Plain atavistic savagery!' Laffler swept his arm in an all-embracing gesture. 'Why do we all sit here at our meat? Not only to appease physical demands, but because our atavistic selves cry for release. Think back, Costain. Do you remember that I once described Sbirro as the epitome of civilization? Can you now see why? A brilliant man, he fully understands the nature of human beings. But unlike lesser men he bends all his efforts to the satisfaction of our innate natures without resultant harm to some innocent bystander.'

'When I think back on the wonders of lamb Amirstan,' said Costain, 'I quite understand what you're driving at. And, by the way, isn't it nearly due to appear on the bill of fare? It must have been over a month ago that it was last served.'

The waiter, filling the tumblers, hesitated. 'I am so sorry, sair. No special this evening.'

'There's your answer,' Laffler grunted, 'and probably just my luck to miss out on it altogether the next time.'

Costain stared at him. 'Oh, come, that's impossible.'

'No, blast it.' Laffler drank off half his water at a gulp and the waiter immediately refilled the glass. 'I'm off to South America for a surprise tour of inspection. One month, two months, Lord knows how long.'

'Are things that bad down there?'

'They could be better.' Laffler suddenly grinned. 'Mustn't forget it takes very mundane dollars and cents to pay the tariff at Sbirro's.'

'I haven't heard a word of this around the office.'

'Wouldn't be a surprise tour if you had. Nobody knows about this except myself – and now you. I want to walk in on them completely unsuspected. Find out what flimflammery they're up to down there. As far as the office is concerned, I'm off on a jaunt somewhere. Maybe recuperating in some sanatorium from my hard work. Anyhow, the business will be in good hands. Yours, among them.'

'Mine?' said Costain, surprised.

'When you go in tomorrow you'll find yourself in receipt of a promotion, even if I'm not there to hand it to you personally. Mind you, it has nothing to do with our friendship either; you've done fine work, and I'm immensely grateful for it.'

Costain reddened under the praise. 'You don't expect to be in tomorrow. Then you're leaving tonight?'

Laffler nodded. 'I've been trying to wangle some reservations. If they come through, well, this will be in the nature of a farewell celebration.'

'You know,' said Costain slowly, 'I devoutly hope that your reservations don't come through. I believe our dinners here have come to mean more to me than I ever dared imagine.'

The waiter's voice broke in. 'Do you wish to be served now, sair?' and they both started.

'Of course, of course,' said Laffler sharply, 'I didn't realize you were waiting.'

'What bothers me,' he told Costain as the waiter turned away, 'is the thought of the lamb Amirstan I'm bound to miss. To tell you the truth, I've already put off my departure a week, hoping to hit a lucky night, and now I simply can't delay any more. I do hope that when you're sitting over your share of lamb Amirstan, you'll think of me with suitable regrets.'

Costain laughed. 'I will indeed,' he said as he turned to his dinner.

Hardly had he cleared the plate when a waiter silently reached for it. It was not their usual waiter, he observed; it was none other than the victim of the assault.

'Well,' Costain said, 'how do you feel now? Still under the weather?'

The waiter paid no attention to him. Instead, with the air of a man under great strain, he turned to Laffler. 'Sair,' he whispered. 'My life. I owe it to you. I can repay you!'

Laffler looked up in amazement, then shook his head firmly. 'No,' he said, 'I want nothing from you, understand? You have repaid me sufficiently with your thanks. Now get on with your work and let's hear no more about it.'

The waiter did not stir an inch, but his voice rose slightly. 'By the body and blood of your God, sair, I will help you even if you do not want! *Do not go into the kitchen, sair*. I trade you my life for yours, sair, when I speak this. Tonight or any night of your life, do not go into the kitchen at Sbirro's!'

Laffler sat back, completely dumbfounded. 'Not go into the kitchen? Why shouldn't I go into the kitchen if Mr Sbirro ever took it into his head to invite me there? What's all this about?'

A hard hand was laid on Costain's back, and another gripped the waiter's arm. The waiter remained frozen to the spot, his lips compressed, his eyes downcast.

'What is all *what* about, gentlemen?' purred the voice. 'So opportune an arrival. In time as ever, I see, to answer all the questions, hurr?'

Laffler breathed a sigh of relief. 'Ah, Sbirro, thank heaven you're here. This man is saying something about my not going into your kitchen. Do you know what he means?'

The teeth showed in a broad grin. 'But of course. This good

man was giving you advice in all amiability. It so happens that
my too emotional chef heard some rumour that I might have a
guest into his precious kitchen, and he flew into a fearful rage.
Such a rage, gentlemen! He even threatened to give notice on the
spot, and you can understand what that would mean to Sbirro's,
hurr? Fortunately, I succeeded in showing him what a signal
honour it is to have an esteemed patron and true connoisseur
observe him at his work firsthand, and now he is quite amenable.
Quite, hurr?'

He released the waiter's arm. 'You are at the wrong table,' he
said softly. 'See that it does not happen again.'

The waiter slipped off without daring to raise his eyes and
Sbirro drew a chair to the table. He seated himself and brushed
his hand lightly over his hair. 'Now I am afraid that the cat is
out of the bag, hurr? This invitation to you, Mr Laffler, was to
be a surprise; but the surprise is gone, and all that is left is the
invitation.'

Laffler mopped beads of perspiration from his forehead. 'Are
you serious?' he said huskily. 'Do you mean that we are really to
witness the preparation of your food tonight?'

Sbirro drew a sharp fingernail along the tablecloth, leaving a
thin, straight line printed in the linen. 'Ah,' he said, 'I am faced
with a dilemma of great proportions.' He studied the line soberly.
'You Mr Laffler, have been my guest for ten long years. But our
friend here – '

Costain raised his hand in protest. 'I understand perfectly. This
invitation is solely to Mr Laffler, and naturally my presence is
embarrassing. As it happens, I have an early engagement for this
evening and must be on my way anyhow. So you see there's no
dilemma at all, really.'

'No,' said Laffler, 'absolutely not. That wouldn't be fair at all.
We've been sharing this until now, Costain, and I won't enjoy
this experience half as much if you're not along. Surely Sbirro
can make his conditions flexible, this one occasion.'

They both looked at Sbirro who shrugged his shoulders
regretfully.

Costain rose abruptly. 'I'm not going to sit here, Laffler, and
spoil your great adventure. And then too,' he bantered, 'think of

that ferocious chef waiting to get his cleaver on you. I prefer not to be at the scene. I'll just say good-bye,' he went on, to cover Laffler's guilty silence, 'and leave you to Sbirro. I'm sure he'll take pains to give you a good show.' He held out his hand and Laffler squeezed it painfully hard.

'You're being very decent, Costain,' he said. 'I hope you'll continue to dine here until we meet again. It shouldn't be too long.'

Sbirro made way for Costain to pass. 'I will expect you,' he said. *'Au'voir.'*

Costain stopped briefly in the dim foyer to adjust his scarf and fix his Homburg at the proper angle. When he turned away from the mirror, satisfied at last, he saw with a final glance that Laffler and Sbirro were already at the kitchen door, Sbirro holding the door invitingly wide with one hand, while the other rested, almost tenderly, on Laffler's meaty shoulders.

The Cat's-Paw

There was little to choose among any of the rooms in the board-
ing house in their dingy, linoleum-floored, brass-bedsteaded uni-
formity, but the day he answered the advertisement on the *Help
Wanted* page, Mr Crabtree realized that one small advantage
accrued to his room: the public telephone in the hallway was
opposite his door, and simply by keeping an ear cocked he could
be at the instrument a moment after the first shrill warning ring
had sounded.

In view of this he closed his application for employment not
only with his signature but with the number of the telephone as
well. His hand shook a little as he did so; he felt party to a gross
deception in implying that the telephone was his personal
property, but the prestige to be gained this way, so he thought,
might somehow weight the balance in his favour. To that end he
tremorously sacrificed the unblemished principles of a life-
time.

The advertisement itself had been nothing less than a miracle.
Man wanted, it said, *for hard work at moderate pay. Sober,
honest, industrious former clerk, age 45–50 preferred. Write all
details. Box 111*; and Mr Crabtree, peering incredulously through
his spectacles, had read it with a shuddering dismay at the
thought of all his fellows, age 45–50, who might be seeking hard
work at moderate pay, and who might have read the same notice
minutes, or perhaps hours, before.

His answer could have served as a model Letter of Application
for Employment. His age was forty-eight, his health excellent.
He was unmarried. He had served one single firm for thirty
years; had served it faithfully and well; had an admirable record
for attendance and punctuality. Unfortunately, the firm had
merged with another and larger; regrettably, many capable

employees had to be released. Hours? Unimportant. His only interest was in doing a good job no matter the time involved. Salary? A matter entirely in the hands of his prospective employer. His previous salary had been fifty dollars per week, but naturally that had come after years of proved worth. Available for an interview at any time. References from the following. The signature. And then, the telephone number.

All this had been written and rewritten a dozen times until Mr Crabtree had been satisfied that every necessary word was there, each word in its proper place. Then, in the copperplate hand that had made his ledgers a thing of beauty, the final draft had been transferred to fine bond paper purchased toward this very contingency, and posted.

After that, alone with his speculations on whether a reply would come by mail, by telephone, or not at all, Mr Crabtree spent two endless and heart-fluttering weeks until the moment when he answered a call and heard his name come over the wire like the crack of doom.

'Yes,' he said shrilly, 'I'm Crabtree! I sent a letter!'

'Calmly, Mr Crabtree, calmly,' said the voice. It was a clear, thin voice, which seemed to pick up and savour each syllable before delivering it, and it had an instant and chilling effect on Mr Crabtree who was clutching the telephone as if pity could be squeezed from it.

'I have been considering your application,' the voice went on with the same painful deliberation, 'and I am most gratified by it. Most gratified. But before calling the matter settled, I should like to make clear the terms of employment I am offering. You would not object to my discussing it now?'

The word *employment* rang dizzily through Mr Crabtree's head. 'No,' he said, 'please do.'

'Very well. First of all, do you feel capable of operating your own establishment?'

'My own establishment?'

'Oh, have no fears about the size of the establishment or the responsibilities involved. It is a matter of some confidential reports which must be drawn up regularly. You would have your own office, your name on the door, and, of course, no supervision directly over you. That should explain the need for an exceptionally reliable man.'

'Yes,' said Mr Crabtree, 'but those confidential reports ...'

'Your office will be supplied with a list of several important corporations. It will also receive subscriptions to a number of financial journals which frequently make mention of those same corporations. You will note all such references as they appear, and, at the end of each day, consolidate them into a report which will be mailed to me. I must add that none of this calls for any theoretical work or literary treatment. Accuracy, brevity, clarity: those are the three measures to go by. You understand that, of course?'

'Yes, indeed,' said Mr Crabtree fervently.

'Excellent,' said the voice. 'Now your hours will be from nine to five, six days a week, with an hour off at noon for lunch. I must stress this: I am insistent on punctuality and attendance, and I expect you to be as conscientious about these things as if you were under my personal supervision every moment of the day. I hope I do not offend you when I emphasize this?'

'Oh, no, sir!' said Mr Crabtree. 'I ...'

'Let me continue,' the voice said. 'Here is the address where you will appear one week from today, and the number of your room' – Mr Crabtree without pencil or paper at hand pressed the numbers frantically into his memory – 'and the office will be completely prepared for you. The door will be open, and you will find two keys in a drawer of the desk: one for the door and one for the cabinet in the office. In the desk you will also find the list I mentioned, as well as the materials needed in making out your reports. In the cabinet you will find a stock of periodicals to start work on.'

'I beg your pardon,' said Mr Crabtree, 'but those reports ...'

'They should contain every single item of interest about the corporations on your list, from business transactions to changes in personnel. And they must be mailed to me immediately upon your leaving the office each day. Is that clear?'

'Only one thing,' said Mr Crabtree. 'To whom – where do I mail them?'

'A pointless question,' said the voice sharply, much to Mr

Crabtree's alarm. 'To the box number with which you are already familiar, of course.'

'Of course,' said Mr Crabtree.

'Now,' said the voice with a gratifying return to its original deliberate tones, 'the question of salary. I have given it a good deal of thought, since as you must realize, there are a number of factors involved. In the end, I let myself be guided by the ancient maxim: a good workman is worthy of his hire – you recall those words?'

'Yes,' said Mr Crabtree.

'And,' the voice said, 'a poor workman can be easily dispensed with. On that basis, I am prepared to offer you fifty-two dollars a week. Is that satisfactory?'

Mr Crabtree stared at the telephone dumbly and then recovered his voice. 'Very,' he gasped. 'Oh, very much so. I must confess I never ...'

The voice brought him up sharply. 'But that is conditional, you understand. You will be – to use a rather clumsy term – on probation until you have proved yourself. Either the job is handled to perfection, or there is no job.'

Mr Crabtree felt his knees turn to water at the grim suggestion. 'I'll do my best,' he said. 'I most certainly will do my absolute best.'

'And,' the voice went on relentlessly, 'I attach great significance to the way you observe the confidential nature of your work. It is not to be discussed with anyone, and since the maintenance of your office and supplies lies entirely in my hands there can be no excuse for a defection. I have also removed temptation in the form of a telephone which you will *not* find on your desk. I hope I do not seem unjust in my abhorrence of the common practice where employees waste their time in idle conversation during working hours.'

Since the death of an only sister twenty years before, there was not a soul in the world who would have dreamed of calling Mr Crabtree to make any sort of conversation whatsoever; but he only said, 'No, sir. Absolutely not.'

'Then you are in agreement with all the terms we have discussed?'

'Yes, sir,' said Mr Crabtree.

'Any further questions?'

'One thing,' said Mr Crabtree. 'My salary. How ...'

'It will reach you at the end of each week,' said the voice, 'in cash. Anything else?'

Mr Crabtree's mind was now a veritable log-jam of questions, but he found it impossible to fix on any particular one. Before he could do so, the voice said crisply, 'Good luck, then,' and there was the click which told him his caller had hung up. It was only when he attempted to do the same that he discovered his hand had been clenched so tightly around the receiver that it cost him momentary anguish to disengage it.

It must be admitted that the first time Mr Crabtree approached the address given him, it would not have surprised him greatly to find no building there at all. But the building was there, reassuring in its immensity, teeming with occupants who packed the banks of elevators solidly, and, in the hallways, looked through him and scurried around him with efficient disinterest.

The office was there too, hidden away at the end of a devious corridor of its own on the very top floor, a fact called to Mr Crabtree's attention by a stairway across the corridor, which led to an open door through which the flat grey of the sky could be seen.

The most impressive thing about the office was the CRABTREE'S AFFILIATED REPORTS boldly stencilled on the door. Opening the door, one entered an incredibly small and narrow room made even smaller by the massive dimensions of the furniture that crowded it. To the right, immediately inside the door, was a gigantic filing cabinet. Thrust tightly against it, but still so large that it utilized the remainder of the wall space on that side, was a huge, old-fashioned desk with a swivel chair before it.

The window set in the opposite wall was in keeping with the furniture. It was an immense window, broad and high, and its sill came barely above Mr Crabtree's knees. He felt a momentary qualm when he first glanced through it and saw the sheer dizzying drop below, the terrifying quality of which was heightened by the blind, windowless walls of the building directly across from him.

One look was enough; henceforth, Mr Crabtree kept the bottom section of the window securely fastened and adjusted only the top section to his convenience.

The keys were in a desk drawer; pen, ink, a box of nibs, a deck of blotters, and a half-dozen other accessories more impressive than useful were in another drawer; a supply of stamps was at hand; and, most pleasant, there was a plentiful supply of stationery, each piece bearing the letterhead, *Crabtree's Affiliated Reports*, the number of the office, and the address of the building. In his delight at this discovery Mr Crabtree dashed off a few practice lines with some bold flourishes of the pen, and then, a bit alarmed at his own prodigality, carefully tore the sheet to minute shreds and dropped it into the waste-basket at his feet.

After that, his efforts were devoted wholly to the business at hand. The filing cabinet disgorged a dismayingly large file of publications which had to be pored over, line by line, and Mr Crabtree never finished studying a page without the harrowing sensation that he had somehow bypassed the mention of a name which corresponded to one on the typed list he had found, as promised, in the desk. Then he would retrace the entire page with an awful sense of dallying at his work, and groan when he came to the end of it without finding what he had not wanted to find in the first place.

It seemed to him at times that he could never possibly deplete the monstrous pile of periodicals before him. Whenever he sighed with pleasure at having made some headway, he would be struck with the gloomy foreknowledge that the next morning would find a fresh delivery of mail at his door and, consequently, more material to add to the pile.

There were, however, breaks in this depressing routine. One was the preparation of the daily report, a task which, somewhat to Mr Crabtree's surprise, he found himself learning to enjoy; the other was the prompt arrival each week of the sturdy envelope containing his salary down to the last dollar bill, although this was never quite the occasion for unalloyed pleasure it might have been.

Mr Crabtree would carefully slit open one end of the envelope, remove the money, count it, and place it neatly in his ancient wallet. Then he would poke trembling exploratory fingers into the envelope, driven by the fearful recollection of his past experience to look for the notice that would tell him his services were no longer required. That was always a bad moment, and it had the unfailing effect of leaving him ill and shaken until he could bury himself in his work again.

The work was soon part of him. He had ceased bothering with the typed list; every name on it was firmly imprinted in his mind, and there were restless nights when he could send himself off to sleep merely by repeating the list a few times. One name in particular had come to intrigue him, merited special attention. *Efficiency Instruments, Ltd* was unquestionably facing stormy weather. There had been drastic changes in personnel, talks of a merger, sharp fluctuations on the market.

It rather pleased Mr Crabtree to discover that with the passage of weeks into months each of the names on his list had taken on a vivid personality for him. *Amalgamated* was steady as a rock, stolid in its comfortable success; *Universal* was high-pitched, fidgety in its exploration of new techniques; and so on down the line. But *Efficiency Instruments Ltd* was Mr Crabtree's pet project, and he had, more than once, nervously caught himself giving it perhaps a shade more attention than it warranted. He brought himself up sharply at such times; impartiality must be maintained, otherwise ...

It came without any warning at all. He returned from lunch, punctual as ever, opened the door of the office, and knew he was standing face to face with his employer.

'Come in, Mr Crabtree,' said the clear, thin voice, 'and shut the door.'

Mr Crabtree closed the door and stood speechless.

'I must be a prepossessing figure,' said the visitor with a certain relish, 'to have such a potent effect on you. You know who I am, of course?'

To Mr Crabtree's numbed mind, the large, bulbous eyes fixed unwinkingly on him, the wide, flexible mouth, the body, short and round as a barrel, bore a horrifying resemblance to a frog sitting comfortably at the edge of a pond, with himself in the unhappy role of a fly hovering close by.

'I believe,' said Mr Crabtree shakily, 'that you are my employer, Mr ... Mr ...'

A stout forefinger nudged Mr Crabtree's ribs playfully. 'As long as the bills are paid, the name is unimportant, eh, Mr Crabtree? However, for the sake of expedience, let me be known to you as – say – George Spelvin. Have you ever encountered the ubiquitous Mr Spelvin in your journeyings, Mr Crabtree?'

'I'm afraid not,' said Mr Crabtree miserably.

'Then you are not a playgoer, and that is all to the good. And if I may hazard a guess, you are not one to indulge yourself in literature or the cinema either?'

'I do try to keep up with the daily newspaper,' said Mr Crabtree stoutly. 'There's a good deal to read in it, you know, Mr Spelvin, and it's not always easy, considering my work here, to find time for other diversions. That is, if a man wants to keep up with the newspapers.'

The corners of the wide mouth lifted in what Mr Crabtree hoped was a smile. 'That is precisely what I hoped to hear you say. Facts, Mr Crabtree, facts! I wanted a man with a single-minded interest in facts, and your words now as well as your application to your work tell me I have found him in you. I am very gratified, Mr Crabtree.'

Mr Crabtree found that the blood was thumping pleasantly through his veins. 'Thank you. Thank you again, Mr Spelvin. I know I've been trying very hard, but I didn't know whether ... Won't you sit down?' Mr Crabtree tried to get his arm around the barrel before him in order to swing the chair into position, and failed. 'The office is a bit small. But very comfortable,' he stammered hastily.

'I am sure it is suitable,' said Mr Spelvin. He stepped back until he was almost fixed against the window and indicated the chair. 'Now I should like you to be seated, Mr Crabtree, while I discuss the matter I came on.'

Under the spell of that commanding hand Mr Crabtree sank into the chair and pivoted it until he faced the window and the squat figure outlined against it. 'If there is any question about today's report,' he said, 'I am afraid it isn't complete yet. There were some notes on *Efficiency Instruments* ...'

Mr Spelvin waved the matter aside indifferently. 'I am not here to discuss that,' he said slowly. 'I am here to find the answer to a problem which confronts me. And I rely on you, Mr Crabtree, to help me find that answer.'

'A problem?' Mr Crabtree found himself warm with a sense of well-being. 'I'll do everything I can to help, Mr Spelvin. Everything I possibly can.'

The bulging eyes probed his worriedly. 'Then tell me this, Mr Crabtree: how would you go about killing a man?'

'I?' said Mr Crabtree. 'How would I go ... I'm afraid I don't understand, Mr Spelvin.'

'I said,' Mr Spelvin repeated, carefully stressing each word, 'how would you go about killing a man?'

Mr Crabtree's jaw dropped. 'But I couldn't. I wouldn't. That,' he said, 'that would be murder!'

'Exactly,' said Mr Spelvin.

'But you're joking,' said Mr Crabtree, and tried to laugh, without managing to get more than a thin, breathless wheeze through his constricted throat. Even that pitiful effort was cut short by the sight of the stony face before him. 'I'm terribly sorry, Mr Spelvin, terribly sorry. You can see it's not the customary ... it's not the kind of thing ...'

'Mr Crabtree. In the financial journals you study so assiduously you will find my name – my own name – repeated endlessly. I have a finger in many pies, Mr Crabtree, and it always prods the plum. To use the more blatant adjectives, I am wealthy and powerful far beyond your wildest dreams – granting that you are capable of wild dreams – and a man does not attain that position by idling his time away on pointless jokes, or in passing the time of day with hirelings. My time is limited, Mr Crabtree. If you cannot answer my question, say so, and let it go at that!'

'I don't believe I can,' said Mr Crabtree piteously.

'You should have said that at once,' Mr Spelvin replied, 'and spared me any moment of choler. Frankly, I did not believe you could answer my question, and if you had, it would have been a most disillusioning experience. You see, Mr Crabtree, I envy, I deeply envy, your serenity of existence where such questions never even enter. Unfortunately, I am not in that position. At one point in my career, I made a mistake, the only mistake that has ever marked my rise to fortune. This, in time, came to the attention of a man who combines ruthlessness and cleverness to a dangerous degree, and I have been in the power of that man since. He is, in fact, a blackmailer, a common blackmailer who has come to set too high a price on his wares, and so, must now pay for them himself.'

'You intend,' said Mr Crabtree hoarsely, 'to kill him?'

Mr Spelvin threw out a plump hand in protest. 'If a fly rested in the palm of that hand,' he said sharply, 'I could not find the power to close my fingers and crush the life from it. To be blunt, Mr Crabtree, I am totally incapable of committing an act of violence, and while that may be an admirable quality in many ways, it is merely an embarrassment now, since the man must certainly be killed.' Mr Spelvin paused. 'Nor is this a task for a paid assassin. If I resorted to one, I would most assuredly be exchanging one blackmailer for another, and that is altogether impractical.' Mr Spelvin paused again. 'So, Mr Crabtree, you can see there is only one conclusion to be drawn: the responsibility for destroying my tormentor rests entirely on you.'

'Me!' cried Mr Crabtree. 'Why, I could never – no, never!'

'Oh, come,' said Mr Spelvin brusquely. 'You are working yourself into a dangerous state. Before you carry it any further, Mr Crabtree, I should like to make it clear that your failure to carry out my request means that when you leave this office today, you leave it permanently. I cannot tolerate an employee who does not understand his position.'

'Not tolerate!' Mr Crabtree. 'But that is not right, that is not right at all, Mr Spelvin. I've been working hard.' His spectacles blurred. He fumbled with them, cleaned them carefully, replaced them on his nose. 'And to leave me with such a secret. I don't see it; I don't see it at all. Why,' he said in alarm, 'it's a matter for the police!'

To his horror Mr Spelvin's face turned alarmingly red, and the huge body started to shake in a convulsion of mirth that rang deafeningly through the room.

'Forgive me,' he managed to gasp at last. 'Forgive me, my dear fellow. I was merely visualizing the scene in which you go to the authorities and tell them of the incredible demands put upon you by your employer.'

'You must understand,' said Mr Crabtree, 'I am not threatening you, Mr Spelvin. It is only …'

'Threatening me? Mr Crabtree, tell me, what connexion do you think there is between us in the eyes of the world?'

'Connexion? I work for you, Mr Spelvin. I'm an employee here. I …'

Mr Spelvin smiled blandly. 'What a curious delusion,' he said, 'when one can see that you are merely a shabby little man engaged in some pitiful little enterprise that could not possibly be of interest to me.'

'But you employed me yourself, Mr Spelvin! I wrote a letter of application!'

'You did,' said Mr Spelvin, 'but unfortunately the position was already filled, as I informed you in my very polite letter of explanation. You look incredulous, Mr Crabtree, so let me inform you that your letter and a copy of my reply rest securely in my files should the matter ever be called to question.'

'But this office! These furnishings! My subscriptions!'

'Mr Crabtree, Mr Crabtree,' said Mr Spelvin shaking his head heavily, 'did *you* ever question the source of your weekly income? The manager of this building, the dealers in supplies, the publishers who deliver their journals to you were no more interested in my identity than you were. It is, I grant, a bit irregular for me to deal exclusively in currency sent through the mails in your name, but have no fears for me, Mr Crabtree. Prompt payments are the opiate of the business man.'

'But my reports!' said Mr Crabtree who was seriously starting to doubt his own existence.

'To be sure, the reports. I daresay that the ingenious Mr Crabtree, after receiving my unfavourable reply to his application, decided to go into business for himself. He thereupon instituted a service of financial reports and even attempted to make *me* one of his clients! I rebuffed him sharply, I can tell you (I have his first report *and* a copy of my reply to it), but he foolishly persists in his efforts. Foolishly, I say, because his reports are absolutely useless to me; I have no interest in any of the corporations he discusses, and why he should imagine I would have is beyond my reckoning. Frankly, I suspect the man is an eccentric of the worst type, but since I have had dealings with many of that type I merely disregard him, and destroy his daily reports on their arrival.'

'Destroy them?' said Mr Crabtree stupefied.

'You have no cause for complaint, I hope,' said Mr Spelvin with some annoyance. 'To find a man of your character, Mr Crabtree, it was necessary for me to specify *hard work* in my advertisement. I am only living up to my part of the bargain in providing it, and I fail to see where the final disposition of it is any of your concern.'

'A man of my character,' echoed Mr Crabtree helplessly, 'to commit murder?'

'And why not?' The wide mouth tightened ominously. 'Let me enlighten you, Mr Crabtree. I have spent a pleasant and profitable share of my life in observing the human species, as a scientist might study insects under glass. And I have come to one conclusion, Mr Crabtree, one above all others which has contributed to the making of my own success. I have come to the conclusion that to the majority of our species it is the function that is important, not the motives, nor the consequences.

'My advertisement, Mr Crabtree, was calculated to enlist the services of one like that; a perfect representative of the type, in fact. From the moment you answered that advertisement to the present, you have been living up to all my expectations: you have been functioning flawlessly with no thought of either motive or consequence.

'Now murder has been made part of your function. I have honoured you with an explanation of its motives; the consequences are clearly defined. Either you continue to function as you always have, or, to put it in a nutshell, you are out of a job.'

'A job!' said Mr Crabtree wildly. 'What does a job matter to a man in prison! Or to a man being hanged!'

'Oh, come,' remarked Mr Spelvin placidly. 'Do you think I'd lead you into a trap which might snare me as well? I am afraid you are being obtuse, my dear man. If you are not, you must realize clearly that my own security is tied in the same package as yours. And nothing less than your permanent presence in this office and your steadfast application to your work is the guarantee of that security.'

'That may be easy to say when you're hiding under an assumed name,' said Mr Crabtree hollowly.

'I assure you, Mr Crabtree, my position in the world is such that my identity can be unearthed with small effort. But I must also remind you that should you carry out my request you will then be a criminal and, consequently, very discreet.

'On the other hand, if you do not carry out my request – and you have complete freedom of choice in that – any charges you may bring against me will be dangerous only to you. The world, Mr Crabtree, knows nothing about our relationship, and nothing about my affair with the gentleman who has been victimizing me and must now become my victim. Neither his demise nor your charges could ever touch me, Mr Crabtree.

'Discovering my identity, as I said, would not be difficult. But using that information, Mr Crabtree, can only lead you to a prison or an institution for the deranged.'

Mr Crabtree felt the last dregs of his strength seeping from him. 'You have thought of everything,' he said.

'Everything, Mr Crabtree. When you entered my scheme of things, it was only to put my plan into operation; but long before that I was hard at work weighing, measuring, evaluating every step of that plan. For example, this room, this very room, has been chosen only after a long and weary search as perfect for my purpose. Its furnishings have been selected and arranged to further that purpose. How? Let me explain that.

'When you are seated at your desk, a visitor is confined to the space I now occupy at the window. The visitor is, of course, the gentleman in question. He will enter and stand here with the window *entirely open* behind him. He will ask you for an envelope a friend has left. This envelope,' said Mr Spelvin tossing one to the desk. 'You will have the envelope in your desk, will find it, and hand it to him. Then, since he is a very methodical man (I have learned that well), he will place the envelope in the inside pocket of his jacket – and at that moment one good thrust will send him out the window. The entire operation should take less than a minute. Immediately after that,' Mr Spelvin said calmly, 'you will close the window to the bottom and return to your work.'

'Someone,' whispered Mr Crabtree, 'the police ...'

'Will find,' said Mr Spelvin, 'the body of some poor unfortunate who climbed the stairs across the hallway and hurled himself from the roof above. And they will know this because inside that envelope secured in his pocket is not what the gentleman in question expects to find there, but a neatly typewritten note explaining the sad affair and its motives, an apology for any inconvenience caused (suicides are great ones for apologies, Mr Crabtree) and a most pathetic plea for a quick and peaceful burial. And,' said Mr Spelvin, gently touching his fingertips together, 'I do not doubt he will get it.'

'What,' Mr Crabtree said, 'what if something went wrong? If the man opened the letter when it was given to him. Or ... if something like that happened?'

Mr Spelvin shrugged. 'In that case the gentleman in question would merely make his way off quietly and approach me directly about the matter. Realize, Mr Crabtree, that anyone in my friend's line of work expects occasional little attempts like this, and, while he may not be inclined to think them amusing, he would hardly venture into some precipitous action that might kill the goose who lays the golden eggs. No, Mr Crabtree, if such a possibility as you suggest comes to pass, it means only that I must reset my trap, and even more ingeniously.'

Mr Spelvin drew a heavy watch from his pocket, studied it, then replaced it carefully. 'My time is growing short, Mr Crabtree. It is not that I find your company wearing, but my man will be making his appearance shortly, and matters must be entirely in your hands at that time. All I require of you is this: when he arrives, the window will be open.' Mr Spelvin thrust it up hard and stood for a moment looking appreciatively at the drop below. 'The envelope will be in your desk.' He opened the drawer and dropped it in, then closed the drawer firmly. 'And at the moment of decision, you are free to act one way or the other.'

'Free?' said Mr Crabtree. 'You said he would ask for the envelope!'

'He will. He will, indeed. But if you indicate that you know nothing about it, he will quietly make his departure, and later communicate with me. And that will be, in effect, a notice of your resignation from my employ.'

Mr Spelvin went to the door and rested one hand on the knob. 'However,' he said, 'if I do *not* hear from him, that will assure me that you have successfully completed your term of probation and are to be henceforth regarded as a capable and faithful employee.'

'But the reports!' said Mr Crabtree. 'You destroy them ...'

'Of course,' said Mr Spelvin, a little surprised. 'But you will continue with your work and send the reports to me as you have always done. I assure you, it does not matter to me that they are meaningless, Mr Crabtree. They are part of a pattern, and your adherence to that pattern, as I have already told you, is the best assurance of my own security.'

The door opened, closed quietly, and Mr Crabtree found himself alone in the room.

The shadow of the building opposite lay heavily on his desk. Mr Crabtree looked at his watch, found himself unable to read it in the growing dimness of the room, and stood up to pull the cord of the light over his head. At that moment a peremptory knock sounded on the door.

'Come in,' said Mr Crabtree.

The door opened on two figures. One was a small, dapper man, the other a bulky police officer who loomed imposingly over his companion. The small man stepped into the office and, with the gesture of a magician pulling a rabbit from a hat, withdrew a large wallet from his pocket, snapped it open to show the gleam of a badge, closed it, and slid it back into his pocket.

'Police,' said the man succinctly. 'Name's Sharpe.'

Mr Crabtree nodded politely. 'Yes?' he said.

'Hope you don't mind,' said Sharpe briskly. 'Just a few questions.'

As if it were a cue, the large policeman came up with an efficient-looking notebook and the stub of a pencil, and stood there poised for action. Mr Crabtree peered over his spectacles at the notebook, and through them at the diminutive Sharpe. 'No,' said Mr Crabtree, 'not at all.'

'You're Crabtree?' said Sharpe, and Mr Crabtree started, then remembered the name on the door.

'Yes,' he said.

Sharpe's cold eyes flickered over him and then took, in the room with a contemptuous glance. 'This your office?'

'Yes,' said Mr Crabtree.

'You in it all afternoon?'

'Since one o'clock,' said Mr Crabtree. 'I go to lunch at twelve and return at one promptly.'

'I'll bet,' said Sharpe, then nodded over his shoulder. 'That door open any time this afternoon?'

'It's always closed while I am working,' said Mr Crabtree.

'Then you wouldn't be able to see anybody going up the stairs across the hall there.'

'No,' replied Mr Crabtree, 'I wouldn't.'

Sharpe looked at the desk, then ran a reflective thumb along his jaw. 'I guess you wouldn't be in a position to see anything happening outside the window either.'

'No, indeed,' said Mr Crabtree. 'Not while I'm at work.'

'Now,' said Sharpe, 'did you *hear* something outside of that window this afternoon? Something out of the ordinary, I mean.'

'Out of the ordinary?' repeated Mr Crabtree vaguely.

'A yell. Somebody yelling. Anything like that?'

Mr Crabtree puckered his brow. 'Why, yes,' he said, 'yes, I did. And not long ago either. It sounded as if someone had been startled – or frightened. Quite loud, too. It's always so quiet here I couldn't help hearing it.'

Sharpe looked over his shoulder and nodded at the policeman who closed his notebook slowly. 'That ties it up,' said Sharpe. 'The guy made the jump, and the second he did it he changed his mind, so he came down hollering all the way. Well,' he said, turning to Mr Crabtree in a burst of confidence, 'I guess you've got a right to know what's going on here. About an hour ago some character jumped off that roof right over your head. Clear case of suicide, note in his pocket and everything, but we like to get all the facts we can.'

'Do you know,' said Mr Crabtree, 'who he was?'

Sharpe shrugged. 'Another guy with too many troubles. Young, good-looking, pretty snappy dresser. Only thing beats me is why a guy who could afford to dress like that would figure he has more troubles than he can handle.'

The policeman in uniform spoke for the first time. 'That letter he left,' he said deferentially, 'sounds like he was a little crazy.'

'You have to be a little crazy to take that way out,' said Sharpe.

'You're a long time dead,' said the policeman heavily.

Sharpe held the doorknob momentarily. 'Sorry to bother you,' he said to Mr Crabtree, 'but you know how it is. Anyhow, you're lucky in a way. Couple of girls downstairs saw him go by and passed right out.' He winked as he closed the door behind him.

Mr Crabtree stood looking at the closed door until the sound of heavy footsteps passed out of hearing. Then he seated himself in the chair and pulled himself closer to the desk. Some magazines and sheets of stationery lay there in mild disarray, and he arranged the magazines in a neat pile, stacking them so that all corners met precisely.

Mr Crabtree picked up his pen, dipped it into the ink bottle, and steadied the paper before him with his other hand.

Efficiency Instruments, Ltd, he wrote carefully, *shows increased activity ...*

Death on Christmas Eve

As a child I had been vastly impressed by the Boerum house. It was fairly new then, and glossy; a gigantic pile of Victorian rickrack, fretwork, and stained glass, flung together in such chaotic profusion that it was hard to encompass in one glance. Standing before it this early Christmas Eve, however, I could find no echo of that youthful impression. The gloss was long since gone; woodwork, glass, metal, all were merged to a dreary grey, and the shades behind the windows were drawn completely so that the house seemed to present a dozen blindly staring eyes to the passerby.

When I rapped my stick sharply on the door, Celia opened it.

'There is a doorbell right at hand,' she said. She was still wearing the long outmoded and badly wrinkled black dress she must have dragged from her mother's trunk, and she looked, more than ever, the image of old Katrin in her later years: the scrawny body, the tightly compressed lips, the colourless hair drawn back hard enough to pull every wrinkle out of her forehead. She reminded me of a steel trap ready to snap down on anyone who touched her incautiously.

I said, 'I am aware that the doorbell has been disconnected, Celia,' and walked past her into the hallway. Without turning my head, I knew that she was glaring at me; then she sniffed once, hard and dry, and flung the door shut. Instantly we were in a murky dimness that made the smell of dry rot about me stick in my throat. I fumbled for the wall switch, but Celia said sharply, 'No! This is not the time for lights.'

I turned to the white blur of her face, which was all I could see of her. 'Celia,' I said, 'spare me the dramatics.'

'There has been a death in this house. You know that.'

'I have good reason to,' I said, 'but your performance now does not impress me.'

'She was my own brother's wife. She was very dear to me.'

I took a step toward her in the murk and rested my stick on her shoulder. 'Celia,' I said, 'as your family's lawyer, let me give you a word of advice. The inquest is over and done with, and you've been cleared. But nobody believed a word of your precious sentiments then, and nobody ever will. Keep that in mind, Celia.'

She jerked away so sharply that the stick almost fell from my hand. 'Is that what you have come to tell me?' she said.

I said, 'I came because I knew your brother would want to see me today. And if you don't mind my saying so, I suggest that you keep to yourself while I talk to him. I don't want any scenes.'

'Then keep away from him yourself!' she cried. 'He was at the inquest. He saw them clear my name. In a little while he will forget the evil he thinks of me. Keep away from him so that he can forget.'

She was at her infuriating worst, and to break the spell I started up the dark stairway, one hand warily on the balustrade. But I heard her follow eagerly behind, and in some eerie way it seemed as if she were not addressing me, but answering the groaning of the stairs under our feet.

'When he comes to me,' she said, 'I will forgive him. At first I was not sure, but now I know. I prayed for guidance, and I was told that life is too short for hatred. So when he comes to me I will forgive him.'

I reached the head of the stairway and almost went sprawling. I swore in annoyance as I righted myself. 'If you're not going to use lights, Celia, you should, at least, keep the way clear. Why don't you get that stuff out of here?'

'Ah,' she said, 'those are all poor Jessie's belongings. It hurts Charlie to see anything of hers, I knew this would be the best thing to do – to throw all her things out.'

Then a note of alarm entered her voice. 'But you won't tell Charlie, will you? You won't tell him?' she said, and kept repeating it on a higher and higher note as I moved away from her, so that when I entered Charlie's room and closed the door behind me it almost sounded as if I had left a bat chittering behind me.

As in the rest of the house, the shades in Charlie's room were drawn to their full length. But a single bulb in the chandelier overhead dazzled me momentarily, and I had to look twice before I saw Charlie sprawled out on his bed with an arm flung over his eyes. Then slowly he came to his feet and peered at me.

'Well,' he said at last, nodding toward the door, 'she didn't give you any light to come up, did she?'

'No,' I said, 'but I know the way.'

'She's like a mole,' he said. 'Gets around better in the dark than I do in the light. She'd rather have it that way too. Otherwise she might look into a mirror and be scared of what she sees there.'

'Yes,' I said, 'she seems to be taking it very hard.'

He laughed short and sharp as a sea-lion barking. 'That's because she's still got the fear in her. All you get out of her now is how she loved Jessie, and how sorry she is. Maybe she figures if she says it enough, people might get to believe it. But give her a little time and she'll be the same old Celia again.'

I dropped my hat and stick on the bed and laid my overcoat beside them. Then I drew out a cigar and waited until he fumbled for a match and helped me to a light. His hand shook so violently that he had hard going for a moment and muttered angrily at himself. Then I slowly exhaled a cloud of smoke toward the ceiling, and waited.

Charlie was Celia's junior by five years, but seeing him then it struck me that he looked a dozen years older. His hair was the same pale blonde, almost colourless so that it was hard to tell if it was greying or not. But his cheeks wore a fine, silvery stubble, and there were huge blue-black pouches under his eyes. And where Celia was braced against a rigid and uncompromising backbone, Charlie sagged, standing or sitting, as if he were on the verge of falling forward. He stared at me and tugged uncertainly at the limp moustache that dropped past the corners of his mouth.

'You know what I wanted to see you about, don't you?' he said.

'I can imagine,' I said, 'but I'd rather have you tell me.'

'I'll put it to you straight,' he said. 'It's Celia. I want to see her get what's coming to her. Not jail. I want the law to take her and kill her, and I want to be there to watch it.'

A large ash dropped to the floor, and I ground it carefully into the rug with my foot. I said, 'You were at the inquest, Charlie;

you saw what happened. Celia's cleared, and unless additional evidence can be produced, she stays cleared.'

'Evidence! My God, what more evidence does anyone need! They were arguing hammer and tongs at the top of the stairs. Celia just grabbed Jessie and threw her down to the bottom and killed her. That's murder, isn't it? Just the same as if she used a gun or poison or whatever she would have used if the stairs weren't handy?'

I sat down wearily in the old leather-bound armchair there and studied the new ash that was forming on my cigar. 'Let me show it to you from the legal angle,' I said, and the monotone of my voice must have made it sound like a well-memorized formula. 'First, there were no witnesses.'

'I heard Jessie scream and I heard her fall,' he said doggedly, 'and when I ran out and found her there, I heard Celia slam her door shut right then. She pushed Jessie and then scuttered like a rat to be out of the way.'

'But you didn't *see* anything. And since Celia claims that she wasn't on the scene, there were no witnesses. In other words, Celia's story cancels out your story, and since you weren't an eyewitness you can't very well make a murder of what might have been an accident.'

He slowly shook his head.

'You don't believe that,' he said. 'You don't really believe that. Because if you do, you can get out now and never come near me again.'

'It doesn't matter what I believe; I'm showing you the legal aspects of the case. What about motivation? What did Celia have to gain from Jessie's death? Certainly there's no money or property involved; she's as financially independent as you are.'

Charlie sat down on the edge of his bed and leaned toward me with his hands resting on his knees. 'No,' he whispered, 'there's no money or property in it.'

I spread my arms helplessly. 'You see?'

'But you know what it is,' he said. 'It's me. First, it was the old lady with her heart trouble any time I tried to call my soul my own. Then when she died and I thought I was free, it was

Celia. From the time I got up in the morning until I went to bed at night, it was Celia every step of the way. She never had a husband or a baby – but she had me!'

I said quietly, 'She's your sister, Charlie. She loves you,' and he laughed that same unpleasant, short laugh.

'She loves me like ivy loves a tree. When I think back now, I still can't see how she did it, but she would just look at me in a certain way and all the strength would go out of me. And it was like that until I met Jessie ... I remember the day I brought Jessie home, and told Celia we were married. She swallowed it, but that look was in her eyes the same as it must have been when she pushed Jessie down those stairs.'

I said, 'But you admitted at the inquest that you never saw her threaten Jessie or do anything to hurt her.'

'Of course I never *saw*! But when Jessie would go around sick to her heart every day and not say a word, or cry in bed every night and not tell me why, I knew damn well what was going on. You know what Jessie was like. She wasn't so smart or pretty, but she was good-hearted as the day was long, and she was crazy about me. And when she started losing all that sparkle in her after only a month, I knew why. I talked to her and I talked to Celia, and both of them just shook their heads. All I could do was go around in circles, but when it happened, when I saw Jessie lying there, it didn't surprise me. Maybe that sounds queer, but it didn't surprise me at all.'

'I don't think it surprised anyone who knows Celia,' I said, 'but you can't make a case out of that.'

He beat his fist against his knee and rocked from side to side. 'What can I do?' he said. 'That's what I need you for – to tell me what to do. All my life I never got around to doing anything because of her. That's what she's banking on now – that I won't do anything, and that she'll get away with it. Then after a while, things'll settle down, and we'll be right back where we started from.'

I said, 'Charlie, you're getting yourself all worked up to no end.'

He stood up and stared at the door, and then at me. 'But I can do something,' he whispered. 'Do you know what?'

He waited with the bright expectancy of one who has asked a clever riddle that he knows will stump the listener. I stood up facing him, and shook my head slowly. 'No,' I said. 'Whatever you're thinking, put it out of your mind.'

'Don't mix me up,' he said. 'You know you can get away with murder if you're as smart as Celia. Don't you think I'm as smart as Celia?'

I caught his shoulders tightly. 'For God's sake, Charlie,' I said, 'don't start talking like that.'

He pulled out of my hands and went staggering back against the wall. His eyes were bright, and his teeth showed behind his drawn lips. 'What should I do?' he cried. 'Forget everything now that Jessie is dead and buried? Sit here until Celia gets tired of being afraid of me and kills me too?'

My years and girth had betrayed me in that little tussle with him, and I found myself short of dignity and breath. 'I'll tell you one thing,' I said. 'You haven't been out of this house since the inquest. It's about time you got out, if only to walk the streets and look around you.'

'And have everybody laugh at me as I go!'

'Try it,' I said, 'and see. Al Sharp said that some of your friends would be at his bar and grill tonight, and he'd like to see you there. That's my advice – for whatever it's worth.'

'It's not worth anything,' said Celia. The door had been opened, and she stood there rigid, her eyes narrowed against the light in the room. Charlie turned toward her, the muscles of his jaw knotting and unknotting.

'Celia,' he said, 'I told you never to come into this room!'

Her face remained impassive. 'I'm not *in* it. I came to tell you that your dinner is ready.'

He took a menacing step toward her. 'Did you have your ear at that door long enough to hear everything I said? Or should I repeat it for you?'

'I heard an ungodly and filthy thing,' she said quietly, 'an invitation to drink and roister while this house is in mourning. I think I have every right to object to that.'

He looked at her incredulously and had to struggle for words. 'Celia,' he said, 'tell me you don't mean that! Only the blackest hypocrite alive or someone insane could say what you've just said, and mean it.'

That struck a spark in her. 'Insane!' she cried. '*You* dare use that word? Locked in your room, talking to yourself, thinking heaven knows what!' She turned to me suddenly. 'You've talked to him. You ought to know. Is it possible that – '

'He is as sane as you, Celia,' I said heavily.

'Then he should know that one doesn't drink in saloons at a time like this. How could you ask him to do it?'

She flung the question at me with such an air of malicious triumph that I completely forgot myself. 'If you weren't preparing to throw out Jessie's belongings, Celia, I would take that question seriously!'

It was a reckless thing to say, and I had instant cause to regret it. Before I could move, Charlie was past me and had Celia's arms in a paralysing grip.

'Did you dare go into her room?' he raged, shaking her savagely. 'Tell me!' And then, getting an immediate answer from the panic in her face, he dropped her arms as if they were red hot, and stood there sagging with his head bowed.

Celia reached out a placating hand toward him. 'Charlie,' she whimpered, 'don't you see? Having her things around bothers you. I only wanted to help you.'

'Where are her things?'

'By the stairs, Charlie. Everything is there.'

He started down the hallway, and with the sound of his uncertain footsteps moving away I could feel my heartbeat slowing down to its normal tempo. Celia turned to look at me, and there was such a raging hatred in her face that I knew only a desperate need to get out of that house at once. I took my things from the bed and started past her, but she barred the door.

'Do you see what you've done?' she whispered hoarsely. 'Now I will have to pack them all over again. It tires me, but I will have to pack them all over again – just because of you.'

'That is entirely up to you, Celia,' I said coldly.

'You,' she said. 'You old fool. It should have been you along with her when I – '

I dropped my stick sharply on her shoulder and could feel her wince under it. 'As your lawyer, Celia,' I said, 'I advise you to exercise your tongue only during your sleep, when you can't be held accountable for what you say.'

She said no more, but I made sure she stayed safely in front of me until I was out in the street again.

From the Boerum house to Al Sharp's Bar and Grill was only a few minutes' walk, and I made it in good time, grateful for the sting of the clear winter air in my face. Al was alone behind the bar, busily polishing glasses, and when he saw me enter he greeted me cheerfully. 'Merry Christmas, counsellor,' he said.

'Same to you,' I said and watched him place a comfortable-looking bottle and a pair of glasses on the bar.

'You're regular as the seasons, counsellor,' said Al, pouring out two stiff ones. 'I was expecting you along right about now.'

We drank to each other and Al leaned confidingly on the bar. 'Just come from there?'

'Yes,' I said.

'See Charlie?'

'And Celia,' I said.

'Well,' said Al, 'that's nothing exceptional. I've seen her too when she comes by to do some shopping. Runs along with her head down and that black shawl over it like she was being chased by something. I guess she is at that.'

'I guess she is,' I said.

'But Charlie, he's the one. Never see him around at all. Did you tell him I'd like to see him some time?'

'Yes,' I said. 'I told him.'

'What did he say?'

'Nothing. Celia said it was wrong for him to come here while he was in mourning.'

Al whistled softly and expressively, and twirled a forefinger at his forehead. 'Tell me,' he said, 'do you think it's safe for them to be alone together like they are? I mean, the way things stand, and the way Charlie feels, there could be another case of trouble there.'

'It looked like it for a while tonight,' I said. 'But it blew over.'

'Until next time,' said Al.

'I'll be there,' I said.

Al looked at me and shook his head. 'Nothing changes in that house,' he said. 'Nothing at all. That's why you can figure out all the answers in advance. That's how I knew you'd be standing here right about now talking to me about it.'

I could still smell the dry rot of the house in my nostrils, and I knew it would take days before I could get it out of my clothes.

'This is one day I'd like to cut out of the calendar permanently,' I said.

'And leave them alone to their troubles. It would serve them right.'

'They're not alone,' I said. 'Jessie is with them. Jessie will always be with them until that house and everything in it is gone.'

Al frowned. 'It's the queerest thing that ever happened in this town, all right. The house all black, her running through the streets like something hunted, him lying there in that room with only the walls to look at, for – when was it Jessie took that fall, counsellor?'

By shifting my eyes a little I could see in the mirror behind Al the reflection of my own face: ruddy, deep jowled, a little incredulous.

'Twenty years ago,' I heard myself saying. 'Just twenty years ago tonight.'

The Orderly World of Mr Appleby

Mr Appleby was a small, prim man who wore rimless spectacles, parted his greying hair in the middle, and took sober pleasure in pointing out that there was no room in the properly organized life for the operations of Chance. Consequently, when he decided that the time had come to investigate the most efficient methods for disposing of his wife he knew where to look.

He found the book, a text on forensic medicine, on the shelf of a second-hand bookshop among several volumes of like topic, and since all but one were in a distressingly shabby and dog-eared state which offended him to his very core, he chose the only one in reasonably good condition. Most of the cases it presented, he discovered on closer examination, were horrid studies of the results (vividly illustrated) of madness and lust – enough to set any decent man wondering at the number of monsters inhabiting the earth. One case, however, seemed to be exactly what he was looking for, and this he made the object of his most intensive study.

It was the case of Mrs X (the book was replete with Mrs X's, and Mr Y's, and Miss Z's) who died after what was presumably an accidental fall on a scatter rug in her home. However, a lawyer representing the interests of the late lamented charged her husband with murder, and at a coroner's investigation was attempting to prove his charge when the accused abruptly settled matters by dropping dead of a heart attack.

All this was of moderate interest to Mr Appleby whose motive, a desire to come into the immediate possession of his wife's estate, was strikingly similar to the alleged motive of Mrs X's husband. But more important were the actual details of the case. Mrs X had been in the act of bringing him a glass of water, said her husband, when the scatter rug, as scatter rugs will, had suddenly slipped from under her feet.

In rebuttal the indefatigable lawyer had produced a medical authority who made clear through a number of charts (all of which were handsomely reproduced in the book) that in the act of receiving the glass of water it would have been child's play for the husband to lay one hand behind his wife's shoulder, another hand along her jaw, and with a sudden thrust produce the same drastic results as the fall on the scatter rug, without leaving any clues as to the nature of his crime.

It should be made clear now that in studying these charts and explanations relentlessly Mr Appleby was not acting the part of the greedy man going to any lengths to appease that greed. True, it was money he wanted, but it was money for the maintenance of what he regarded as a holy cause. And that was the Shop: *Appleby, Antiques and Curios.*

The Shop was the sun of Mr Appleby's universe. He had bought it twenty years before with the pittance left by his father, and at best it provided him with a poor living. At worst – and it was usually at worst – it had forced him to draw on his mother's meagre store of good will and capital. Since his mother was not one to give up a penny lightly, the Shop brought about a series of pitched battles which, however, always saw it the victor – since in the last analysis the Shop was to Mr Appleby what Mr Appleby was to his mother.

This unhappy triangle was finally shattered by his mother's death, at which time Mr Appleby discovered that she had played a far greater role in maintaining his orderly little world than he had hitherto realized. This concerned not only the money she occasionally gave him, but also his personal habits.

He ate lightly and warily. His mother had been adept at toasting and boiling his meals to perfection. His nerves were violently shaken if anything in the house was out of place, and she had been a living assurance he would be spared this. Her death, therefore, left a vast and uncomfortable gap in his life, and in studying methods to fill it he was led to contemplate marriage, and then to the act itself.

His wife was a pale, thin-lipped woman so much like his mother in appearance and gesture that sometimes on her entrance into a room he was taken aback by the resemblance. In only one respect did she fail him: she could not understand the significance of the Shop, nor his feelings about it. That was disclosed the first time he broached the subject of a small loan that would enable him to meet some business expenses.

Mrs Appleby had been well in the process of withering on the vine when her husband-to-be had proposed to her, but to give her full due she was not won by the mere prospect of finally making a marriage. Actually, though she would have blushed at such a blunt statement of her secret thought, it was the large, mournful eyes behind his rimless spectacles that turned the trick, promising, as they did, hidden depths of emotion neatly garbed in utter respectability. When she learned very soon after her wedding that the hidden depths were evidently too well hidden ever to be explored by her, she shrugged the matter off and turned to boiling and toasting his meals with good enough grace. The knowledge that the impressive *Appleby, Antiques and Curios* was a hollow shell she took in a different spirit.

She made some brisk investigations and then announced her findings to Mr Appleby with some heat.

'Antiques and curios!' she said shrilly. 'Why, that whole collection of stuff is nothing but a pile of junk. Just a bunch of worthless dust-catchers, that's all it is!'

What she did not understand was that these objects, which to the crass and commercial eye might seem worthless, were to Mr Appleby the stuff of life itself. The Shop had grown directly from his childhood mania for collecting, assorting, labelling, and preserving anything he could lay his hands on. And the value of any item in the Shop increased proportionately with the length of time he possessed it; whether a cracked imitation of Sèvres, or clumsily faked Chippendale, or rusty sabre made no difference. Each piece had won a place for itself; a permanent, immutable place, as far as Mr Appleby was concerned; and strangely enough it was the sincere agony he suffered in giving up a piece that led to the few sales he made. The customer who was uncertain of values had only to get a glimpse of this agony to be convinced that he was getting a rare bargain. Fortunately, no customer could have imagined for a moment that it was the thought of the empty space left by the object's departure – the brief disorder which the emptiness made – and not a passion for the object itself that drew Mr Appleby's pinched features into a mask of pain.

So, not understanding, Mrs Appleby took an unsympathetic tack. 'You'll get my mite when I'm dead and gone,' she said, 'and only when I'm dead and gone.'

Thus unwittingly she tried herself, was found wanting, and it only remained for sentence to be executed. When the time came Mr Appleby applied the lessons he had gleaned from his invaluable textbook and found them accurate in every detail. It was over quickly, quietly, and, outside of a splash of water on his trousers, neatly. The Medical Examiner growled something about those indescribable scatter rugs costing more lives than drunken motorists; the policeman in charge kindly offered to do whatever he could in the way of making funeral arrangements; and that was all there was to it.

It had been so easy – so undramatic, in fact – that it was not until a week later when a properly sympathetic lawyer was making him an accounting of his wife's estate that Mr Appleby suddenly understood the whole, magnificent new world that had been opened up to him.

Discretion must sometimes outweigh sentiment, and Mr Appleby was, if anything, a discreet man. After his wife's estate had been cleared, the Shop was moved to another location far from its original setting. It was moved again after the sudden demise of the second Mrs Appleby, and by the time the sixth Mrs Appleby had been disposed of, the removals were merely part of a fruitful pattern.

Because of their similarities – they were all pale, thin-featured women with pinched lips, adept at toasting and boiling, and adamant on the subjects of regularity and order – Mr Appleby was inclined to remember his departed wives rather vaguely *en masse*. Only in one regard did he qualify them: the number of digits their bank accounts totalled up to. For that reason he thought of the first two Mrs Applebys as Fours; the third as a Three (an unpleasant surprise); and the last three as Fives. The sum would have been a pretty penny by anyone else's standards, but since each succeeding portion of it had been snapped up by the insatiable *Appleby, Antiques and Curios* – in much the way a fly is snapped up by a hungry lizard – Mr Appleby found himself soon after the burial of the sixth Mrs Appleby in deeper and warmer financial waters than ever. So desperate were his circumstances that although he dreamed of another Five he would have settled for a Four on the spot. It was at this opportune moment that Martha Sturgis entered his life, and after fifteen minutes' conversation with her he brushed all thoughts of Fours and Fives from his mind.

Martha Sturgis, it seemed, was a Six.

It was not only in the extent of her fortune that she broke the pattern established by the women of Mr Appleby's previous experience. Unlike them, Martha Sturgis was a large, rather shapeless woman who in person, dress, and manner might almost be called (Mr Appleby shuddered a little at the word) blowsy.

It was remotely possible that properly veneered, harnessed, coiffured, and apparelled she might have been made into something presentable, but from all indications Martha Sturgis was a woman who went out of her way to defy such conventions. Her hair, dyed a shocking orange-red, was piled carelessly on her head; her blobby features were recklessly powdered and painted entirely to their disadvantage; her clothes, obviously worn for comfort, were, at the same time, painfully garish; and her shoes gave evidence of long and pleasurable wear without corresponding care being given to their upkeep.

Of all this and its effect on the beholder Martha Sturgis seemed totally unaware. She strode through *Appleby, Antiques and Curios* with an energy that set movable objects dancing in their places; she smoked incessantly, lighting one cigarette from another, while Mr Appleby fanned the air before his face and coughed suggestively; and she talked without pause, loudly and in a deep, hoarse voice that dinned strangely in a Shop so accustomed to the higher, thinner note.

In the first fourteen minutes of their acquaintance, the one quality she displayed that led Mr Appleby to modify some of his immediate revulsion even a trifle was the care with which she priced each article. She examined, evaluated, and cross-examined in detail before moving on with obvious disapproval, and he moved along with her with mounting assurance that he could get her out of the Shop before any damage was done to the stock or his patience. And then in the fifteenth minute she spoke the Word.

'I've got half a million dollars in the bank,' Martha Sturgis remarked with cheerful contempt, 'but I never thought I'd get around to spending a nickel of it on this kind of stuff.'

Mr Appleby had his hand before his face preparatory to waving aside some of the tobacco smoke that eddied about him. In the time it took the hand to drop nervelessly to his side his mind attacked an astonishing number of problems. One concerned the important finger on her left hand which was ringless; the others concerned certain mathematical problems largely dealing with short-term notes, long-term notes, and rates of interest. By the time the hand touched his side, the problems, as far as Mr Appleby was concerned, were well on the way to solution.

And it may be noted there was an added fillip given the matter by the very nature of Martha Sturgis's slovenly and strident being. Looking at her after she had spoken the Word, another man might perhaps have seen her through the sort of veil that a wise photographer casts over the lens of his camera in taking the picture of a prosperous, but unprepossessing, subject. Mr Appleby, incapable of such self-deceit, girded himself instead with the example of the man who carried a heavy weight on his back for the pleasure it gave him in laying it down. Not only would the final act of a marriage to Martha Sturgis solve important mathematical problems, but it was an act he could play out with the gusto of a man ridding the world of an unpleasant object.

Therefore he turned his eyes, more melancholy and luminous than ever, on her and said, 'It's a great pity, Mrs ...'

She told him her name, emphasizing the *Miss* before it, and Mr Appleby smiled apologetically.

'Of course. As I was saying, it's a great pity when someone of refinement and culture – ' (the *like yourself* floated delicately unsaid on the air) '– should never have known the joy in possession of fine works of art. But, as we all learn, it is never too late to begin, is it?'

Martha Sturgis looked at him sharply and then laughed a

hearty bellow of laughter that stabbed his eardrums painfully. For a moment Mr Appleby, a man not much given to humour, wondered darkly if he had unwittingly uttered something so excruciatingly epigrammatic that it was bound to have this alarming effect.

'My dear man,' said Martha Sturgis, 'if it is your idea that I am here to start cluttering up my life with your monstrosities, perish the thought. What I'm here for is to buy a gift for a friend, a thoroughly infuriating and loathsome person who happens to have the nature and disposition of a bar of stainless steel. I can't think of a better way of showing my feelings toward her than by presenting her with almost anything displayed in your shop. If possible, I should like delivery arranged so that I can be on the scene when she receives the package.'

Mr Appleby staggered under this, then rallied valiantly. 'In that case,' he said, and shook his head firmly, 'it is out of the question. Completely out of the question.'

'Nonsense,' Martha Sturgis said. 'I'll arrange for delivery myself if you can't handle it. Really, you ought to understand that there's no point in doing this sort of thing unless you're on hand to watch the results.'

Mr Appleby kept tight rein on his temper. 'I am not alluding to the matter of delivery,' he said. 'What I am trying to make clear is that I cannot possibly permit anything in my Shop to be bought in such a spirit. Not for any price you could name.'

Martha Sturgis's heavy jaw dropped. 'What was that you said?' she asked blankly.

It was a perilous moment, and Mr Appleby knew it. His next words could set her off into another spasm of that awful laughter that would devastate him completely; or, worse, could send her right out of the Shop forever; or could decide the issue in his favour then and there. But it was a moment that had to be met, and, thought Mr Appleby desperately, whatever else Martha Sturgis might be, she was a Woman.

He took a deep breath. 'It is the policy of this Shop,' he said quietly, 'never to sell anything unless the prospective purchaser shows full appreciation for the article to be bought and can assure it the care and devotion to which it is entitled. That has always been the policy, and always will be as long as I am here. Anything other than that I would regard as desecration.'

He watched Martha Sturgis with bated breath. There was a chair nearby, and she dropped into it heavily so that her skirts were drawn tight by her widespread thighs, and the obscene shoes were displayed mercilessly. She lit another cigarette, regarding him meanwhile with narrowed eyes through the flame of the match, and then fanned the air a little to dispel the cloud of smoke.

'You know,' she said, 'this is very interesting. I'd like to hear more about it.'

To the inexperienced the problem of drawing information of the most personal nature from a total stranger would seem a perplexing one. To Mr Appleby, whose interests had so often been dependent on such information, it was no problem at all. In very short time he had evidence that Martha Sturgis's estimate of her fortune was quite accurate, that she was apparently alone in the world without relatives or intimate friends, and – that she was not averse to the idea of marriage.

This last he drew from her during her now regular visits to the Shop where she would spread herself comfortably on a chair and talk to him endlessly. Much of her talk was about her father to whom Mr Appleby evidently bore a striking resemblance.

'He even dressed like you,' Martha Sturgis said reflectively. 'Neat as a pin, and not only about himself either. He used to make an inspection of the house every day – march through and make sure everything was exactly where it had to be. And he kept it up right to the end. I remember an hour before he died how he went about straightening pictures on the wall.'

Mr Appleby, who had been peering with some irritation at a picture that hung slightly awry on the Shop wall, turned his attentions reluctantly from it.

'And you were with him to the end?' he asked sympathetically.

'Indeed I was.'

'Well,' Mr Appleby said brightly, 'one does deserve some reward for such sacrifice, doesn't one? Especially – and I hope this will not embarrass you, Miss Sturgis – when one considers that such a woman as yourself could undoubtedly have left the care of an aged father to enter matrimony almost at will. Isn't that so?'

Martha Sturgis sighed. 'Maybe it is, and maybe it isn't,' she said, 'and I won't deny that I've had my dreams. But that's all they are, and I suppose that's all they ever will be.'

'Why?' asked Mr Appleby encouragingly.

'Because,' said Martha Sturgis sombrely, 'I have never yet met the man who could fit those dreams. I am not a simpering school-girl, Mr Appleby; I don't have to balance myself against my bank account to know why any man would devote himself to me, and, frankly, his motives would be of no interest. But he must be a decent, respectable man who would spend every moment of his life worrying about me and caring for me; and he must be a man who would make the memory of my father a living thing.'

Mr Appleby rested a hand lightly on her shoulder.

'Miss Sturgis,' he said gravely, 'you may yet meet such a man.'

She looked at him with features that were made even more blobby and unattractive by her emotion.

'Do you mean that, Mr Appleby?' she asked. 'Do you really believe that?'

Faith glowed in Mr Appleby's eyes as he smiled down at her. 'He may be closer than you dare realize,' he said warmly.

Experience had proved to Mr Appleby that once the ice is broken the best thing to do is take a deep breath and plunge in. Accordingly, he let very few days elapse before he made his proposal.

'Miss Sturgis,' he said, 'there comes a time to every lonely man when he can no longer bear his loneliness. If at such a time he is fortunate enough to meet the one woman to whom he could give unreservedly all his respect and tender feelings, he is a fortunate man indeed. Miss Sturgis – I am that man.'

'Why, Mr Appleby!' said Martha Sturgis, colouring a trifle. 'That's really very good of you, but ...'

At this note of indecision his heart sank. 'Wait!' he interposed hastily. 'If you have any doubts, Miss Sturgis, please speak them now so that I may answer them. Considering the state of my emotions, that would only be fair, wouldn't it?'

'Well, I suppose so,' said Martha Sturgis. 'You see, Mr Appleby, I'd rather not get married at all than take the chance of getting someone who wasn't prepared to give me exactly what I'm looking for in marriage: absolute, single-minded devotion all the rest of my days.'

'Miss Sturgis,' said Mr Appleby solemnly, 'I am prepared to give you no less.'

'Men say these things so easily,' she sighed. 'But – I shall certainly think about it, Mr Appleby.'

The dismal prospect of waiting an indefinite time for a woman of such careless habits to render a decision was not made any lighter by the sudden receipt a few days later of a note peremptorily requesting Mr Appleby's presence at the offices of Gainsborough, Gainsborough, and Golding, attorneys-at-law. With his creditors closing in like a wolf pack, Mr Appleby could only surmise the worst, and he was pleasantly surprised upon his arrival at Gainsborough, Gainsborough and Golding to find that they represented, not his creditors, but Martha Sturgis herself.

The elder Gainsborough, obviously very much the guiding spirit of the firm, was a short, immensely fat man with pendulous dewlaps that almost concealed his collar, and large fishy eyes that goggled at Mr Appleby. The younger Gainsborough was a duplicate of his brother, with jowls not quite so impressive, while Golding was an impassive young man with a hatchet face.

'This,' said the elder Gainsborough, his eyes fixed glassily on Mr Appleby, 'is a delicate matter. Miss Sturgis, an esteemed client – ' the younger Gainsborough nodded at this – 'has mentioned entering matrimony with you, sir.'

Mr Appleby sitting primly on his chair was stirred by a pleased excitement. 'Yes?' he said.

'And,' continued the elder Gainsborough, 'while Miss Sturgis is perfectly willing to concede that her fortune may be the object of attraction in any suitor's eyes – ' he held up a pudgy hand to cut short Mr Appleby's shocked protest – 'she is also willing to dismiss that issue – '

'To ignore it, set it aside,' said the younger Gainsborough sternly.

'– if the suitor is prepared to meet all other expectations in marriage.'

'I am,' said Mr Appleby fervently.

'Mr Appleby,' said the elder Gainsborough abruptly, 'have you been married before?'

Mr Appleby thought swiftly. Denial would make any chance word about his past a deadly trap; admission, on the other hand, was a safeguard against that, and a thoroughly respectable one.

'Yes,' he said.

'Divorced?'

'Good heavens, no!' said Mr Appleby, genuinely shocked.

The Gainsboroughs looked at each other in approval. 'Good,' said the elder, 'very good. Perhaps, Mr Appleby, the question seemed impertinent, but in these days of moral laxity ...'

'I should like it known in that case,' said Mr Appleby sturdily, 'that I am as far from moral laxity as any human being can be. Tobacco, strong drink, and – ah – '

'Loose women,' said the younger Gainsborough briskly.

'Yes,' said Mr Appleby reddening, '– are unknown to me.'

The elder Gainsborough nodded. 'Under any conditions,' he said, 'Miss Sturgis will not make any precipitate decision. She should have her answer for you within a month, however, and during that time, if you don't mind taking the advice of an old man, I suggest that you court her assiduously. She is a woman, Mr Appleby, and I imagine that all women are much alike.'

'I imagine they are,' said Mr Appleby.

'Devotion,' said the younger Gainsborough. 'Constancy. That's the ticket.'

What he was being asked to do, Mr Appleby reflected in one of his solitary moments, was to put aside the Shop and the orderly world it represented and to set the unappealing figure of Martha Sturgis in its place. It was a temporary measure, of course; it was one that would prove richly rewarding when Martha Sturgis had been properly wed and sent the way of the preceding Mrs Applebys; but it was not made any easier by enforced familiarity with the woman. It was inevitable that since Mr Appleby viewed matters not only as a prospective bridegroom, but also as a prospective widower, so to speak, he found his teeth constantly set on edge by the unwitting irony which crept into so many of her tedious discussions on marriage.

'The way I see it,' Martha Sturgis once remarked, 'is that a man who would divorce his wife would divorce any other woman he ever married. You take a look at all these broken marriages today, and I'll bet that in practically every case you'll find a man who's always shopping around and never finding what he wants. Now, the man *I* marry,' she said pointedly, 'must be willing to settle down and stay settled.'

'Of course,' said Mr Appleby.

'I have heard,' Martha Sturgis told him on another, and particularly trying, occasion, 'that a satisfactory marriage increases a woman's span of years. That's an excellent argument for marriage, don't you think?'

'Of course,' said Mr Appleby.

It seemed to him that during that month of trial most of his conversation was restricted to the single phrase 'of course', delivered with varying inflections; but the tactic must have been the proper one since at the end of the month he was able to change the formula to 'I do', in a wedding ceremony at which Gainsborough, Gainsborough, and Golding were the sole guests.

Immediately afterward, Mr Appleby (to his discomfort) was borne off with his bride to a photographer's shop where innumerable pictures were made under the supervision of the dour Golding, following which, Mr Appleby (to his delight) exchanged documents with his wife which made them each other's heirs to all properties, possessions, *et cetera*, whatsoever.

If Mr Appleby had occasionally appeared rather abstracted during these festivities, it was only because his mind was neatly arranging the programme of impending events. The rug (the very same one that had served so well in six previous episodes) had to be placed; and then there would come the moment when he would ask for a glass of water, when he would place one hand on her shoulder, and with the other ... It could not be a moment that took place without due time passing; yet it could not be forestalled too long in view of the pressure exercised by the

Shop's voracious creditors. Watching the pen in his wife's hand as she signed her will, he decided there would be time within a few weeks. With the will in his possession there would be no point in waiting longer than that.

Before the first of those weeks was up, however, Mr Appleby knew that even this estimate would have to undergo drastic revision. There was no question about it: he was simply not equipped to cope with his marriage.

For one thing, her home (and now his), a brown-stone cavern inherited from her mother, was a nightmare of disorder. On the principle, perhaps, that anything flung casually aside was not worth picking up since it would only be flung aside again, an amazing litter had accumulated in every room. The contents of brimming closets and drawers were recklessly exchanged, mislaid, or added to the general litter, and over all lay a thin film of dust. On Mr Appleby's quivering nervous system all this had the effect of a fingernail dragging along an endless blackboard.

The one task to which Mrs Appleby devoted herself, as it happened, was the one which her husband prayerfully wished she would spare herself. She doted on cookery, and during mealtimes would trudge back and forth endlessly between kitchen and dining-room laden with dishes outside any of Mr Appleby's experience.

At his first feeble protests his wife had taken pains to explain in precise terms that she was sensitive to any criticism of her cooking, even the implied criticism of a partly emptied plate; and thereafter Mr Appleby plunging hopelessly through rare meats, rich sauces, and heavy pastries, found added to his tribulations the incessant pangs of dyspepsia. Nor were his pains eased by his wife's insistence that he prove himself a trencherman of her mettle. She would thrust plates heaped high with indigestibles under his quivering nose, and, bracing himself like a martyr facing the lions, Mr Appleby would empty his portion into a digestive tract that cried for simple fare properly boiled or toasted.

It became one of his fondest waking dreams, that scene where he returned from his wife's burial to dine on hot tea and toast and, perhaps, a medium-boiled egg. But even that dream and its sequel – where he proceeded to set the house in order – were not sufficient to buoy him up each day when he awoke and reflected on what lay ahead of him.

Each day found his wife more insistent in her demands for his attentions. And on that day when she openly reproved him for devoting more of those attentions to the Shop than to herself, Mr Appleby knew the time had come to prepare for the final act. He brought home the rug that evening and carefully laid it in place between the living room and the hallway that led to the kitchen. Martha Appleby watched him without any great enthusiasm.

'That's a shabby-looking thing, all right,' she said. 'What is it, Appie, an antique or something?'

She had taken to calling him by that atrocious name and seemed cheerfully oblivious to the way he winced under it. He winced now.

'It is not an antique,' Mr Appleby admitted, 'but I hold it dear for many reasons. It has a great deal of sentimental value to me.'

Mrs Appleby smiled fondly at him. 'And you brought it for me, didn't you?'

'Yes,' said Mr Appleby, 'I did.'

'You're a dear,' said Mrs Appleby. 'You really are.'

Watching her cross the rug on slipshod feet to use the telephone, which stood on a small table the other side of the hallway, Mr Appleby toyed with the idea that since she used the telephone at about the same time every evening he could schedule the accident for that time. The advantages were obvious: since those calls seemed to be the only routine she observed with any fidelity, she would cross the rug at a certain time, and he would be in a position to settle matters then and there.

However, thought Mr Appleby as he polished his spectacles, that brought up the problem of how best to approach her under such circumstances. Clearly the tried and tested methods were best, but if the telephone call and the glass of water could be synchronized. ...

'A penny for your thoughts, Appie,' said Mrs Appleby brightly. She had laid down the telephone and crossed the hallway so that she stood squarely on the rug. Mr Appleby replaced his spectacles and peered at her through them.

'I wish,' he said querulously, 'you would not address me by that horrid name. You know how I detest it.'

'Nonsense,' his wife said briefly. 'I think it's cute.'

'I do not.'

'Well, I like it,' said Mrs Appleby with the air of one who has settled a matter once and for all. 'Anyhow,' she pouted, 'that couldn't have been what you were thinking about before I started talking to you, could it?'

It struck Mr Appleby that when this stout, unkempt woman pouted, she resembled nothing so much as a wax doll badly worn by time and handling. He pushed away the thought to frame some suitable answer.

'As it happens,' he said, 'my mind was on the disgraceful state of my clothes. Need I remind you again that there are buttons missing from practically every garment I own?'

Mrs Appleby yawned broadly. 'I'll get to it sooner or later.'

'Tomorrow perhaps?'

'I doubt it,' said Mrs Appleby. She turned toward the stairs. 'Come to sleep, Appie. I'm dead tired.'

Mr Appleby followed her thoughtfully. Tomorrow, he knew, he would have to get one of his suits to the tailor if he wanted to have anything fit to wear at the funeral.

He had brought home the suit and hung it neatly away; he had eaten his dinner; and he had sat in the living room listening to his wife's hoarse voice go on for what seemed interminable hours, although the clock was not yet at nine.

Now with rising excitement he saw her lift herself slowly from her chair and cross the room to the hallway. As she reached for the telephone Mr Appleby cleared his throat sharply. 'If you don't mind,' he said, 'I'd like a glass of water.'

Mrs Appleby turned to look at him. 'A glass of water?'

'If you don't mind,' said Mr Appleby, and waited as she hesitated, then set down the telephone, and turned toward the kitchen. There was the sound of a glass being rinsed in the kitchen, and then Mrs Appleby came up to him holding it out. He laid one hand appreciatively on her plump shoulder, and then lifted the other as if to brush back a strand of untidy hair at her cheek.

'Is that what happened to all the others?' said Mrs Appleby quietly.

Mr Appleby felt his hand freeze in mid-air and the chill from it run down into his marrow. 'Others?' he managed to say. 'What others?'

His wife smiled grimly at him, and he saw that the glass of water in her hand was perfectly steady. 'Six others,' she said. 'That is, six by my count. Why? Were there any more?'

'No,' he said, then caught wildly at himself. 'I don't understand what you're talking about!'

'Dear Appie. Surely you couldn't forget six wives just like that. Unless, of course, I've come to mean so much to you that you can't bear to think of the others. That would be a lovely thing to happen, wouldn't it?'

'I *was* married before,' Mr Appleby said loudly. 'I made that quite clear myself. But this talk about six wives!'

'Of course you were married before, Appie. And it was quite easy to find out to whom – and it was just as easy to find out about the one before that – and all the others. Or even about your mother, or where you went to school, or where you were born. You see, Appie, Mr Gainsborough is really a very clever man.'

'Then it was Gainsborough who put you up to this!'

'Not at all, you foolish little man,' his wife said contemptuously. 'All the time you were making your plans I was unmaking them. From the moment I laid eyes on you I knew you for what you are. Does that surprise you?'

Mr Appleby struggled with the emotions of a man who has picked up a twig to find a viper in his hand. 'How could you know?' he gasped.

'Because you were the image of my father. Because in everything – the way you dress, your insufferable neatness, your priggish arrogance, the little moral lectures you dote on – you are what he was. And all my life I hated him for what he was, and what it did to my mother. He married her for her money, made her every day a nightmare, and then killed her for what was left of her fortune.'

'Killed her?' said Mr Appleby, stupefied.

'Oh, come,' his wife said sharply. 'Do you think you're the

only man who was ever capable of that? Yes, he killed her –
murdered her, if you prefer – by asking for a glass of water, and
then breaking her neck when she offered it to him. A method
strangely similar to yours, isn't it?'

Mr Appleby found the incredible answer rising to his mind,
but refused to accept it. 'What happened to him?' he demanded.
'Tell me what happened! Was he caught?'

'No, he was never caught. There were no witnesses to what he
did, but Mr Gainsborough had been my mother's lawyer, a dear
friend of hers. He had suspicions and demanded a hearing. He
brought a doctor to the hearing who made it plain how my father
could have killed her and made it look as if she had slipped on the
rug, but before there was any decision my father died of a heart
attack.'

'That was the case – the case I read!' Mr Appleby groaned,
and then was silent under his wife's sardonic regard.

'When he was gone,' she went on inexorably, 'I swore I would
some day find a man exactly like him, and I would make that
man live the life my father should have lived. I would know his
every habit and every taste, and none of them should go satisfied.
I would know he married me for my money, and he would never
get a penny of it until I was dead and gone. And that would be a
long, long time, because he would spend his life taking care that
I should live out my life to the last possible breath.'

Mr Appleby pulled his wits together, and saw that despite her
emotion she had remained in the same position. 'How can you
make him do that?' he asked softly, and moved an inch closer.

'It does sound strange, doesn't it, Appie?' she observed. 'But
hardly as strange as the fact that your six wives died by slipping
on a rug – very much like this one – while bringing you a glass of
water – very much like this one. So strange, that Mr Gainsborough was led to remark that too many coincidences will certainly hang a man. Especially if there is reason to bring them to
light in a trial for murder.'

Mr Appleby suddenly found the constriction of his collar unbearable. 'That doesn't answer my question,' he said craftily.
'How can you make sure that I would devote my life to prolong-
ing yours?'

'A man whose wife is in a position to have him hanged should be able to see that clearly.'

'No,' said Mr Appleby in a stifled voice, 'I only see that such a man is forced to rid himself of his wife as quickly as possible.'

'Ah, but that's where the arrangements come in.'

'Arrangements? What arrangements?' demanded Mr Appleby.

'I'd like very much to explain them,' his wife said. 'In fact, I see the time has come when it's imperative to do so. But I do find it uncomfortable standing here like this.'

'Never mind that,' said Mr Appleby impatiently, and his wife shrugged.

'Well, then,' she said coolly, 'Mr Gainsborough now has all the documents about your marriages – the way the previous deaths took place, the way you always happened to get the bequests at just the right moment to pay your shop's debts.

'Besides this, he has a letter from me, explaining that in the event of my death an investigation be made immediately and all necessary action be taken. Mr Gainsborough is really very efficient. The fingerprints and photographs. ...'

'Fingerprints and photographs!' cried Mr Appleby.

'Of course. After my father's death it was found that he had made all preparations for a quick trip abroad. Mr Gainsborough has assured me that in case you had such ideas in your mind you should get rid of them. No matter where you are, he said, it will be quite easy to bring you back again.'

'What do you want of me?' asked Mr Appleby numbly. 'Surely you don't expect me to stay now, and – '

'Oh, yes, I do. And since we've come to this point I may as well tell you I expect you to give up your useless shop once and for all, and make it a point to be at home with me the entire day.'

'Give up the Shop!' he exclaimed.

'You must remember, Appie, that in my letter asking for a full investigation at my death, I did not specify death by any particular means. I look forward to a long and pleasant life with you always at my side, and perhaps – mind you, I only say *perhaps* – some day I shall turn over that letter and all the evidence to you. You can see how much it is to your interest, therefore, to watch over me very carefully.'

The telephone rang with abrupt violence, and Mrs Appleby nodded toward it. 'Almost as carefully,' she said softly, 'as Mr Gainsborough. Unless I call him every evening at nine to report I am well and happy, it seems he will jump to the most shocking conclusions.'

'Wait,' said Mr Appleby. He lifted the telephone and there was no mistaking the voice that spoke.

'Hello,' said the elder Gainsborough. 'Hello, Mrs Appleby?'

Mr Appleby essayed a cunning move. 'No,' he said, 'I'm afraid she can't speak to you now. What is it?'

The voice in his ear took on an unmistakable cold menace. 'This is Gainsborough, Mr Appleby, and I wish to speak to your wife immediately. I will give you ten seconds to have her at this telephone, Mr Appleby. Do you understand?'

Mr Appleby turned dully toward his wife and held out the telephone. 'It's for you,' he said, and then saw with a start of terror that as she turned to set down the glass of water the rug skidded slightly under her feet. Her arms flailed the air as she fought for balance, the glass smashed at his feet drenching his neat trousers, and her face twisted into a silent scream. Then her body struck the floor and lay inertly in the position with which he was so familiar.

Watching her, he was barely conscious of the voice emerging tinnily from the telephone in his hand.

'The ten seconds are up, Mr Appleby,' it said shrilly. 'Do you understand? *Your time is up!*'

Fool's Mate

When George Huneker came home from the office that evening he was obviously fired by a strange excitement. His ordinarily sallow cheeks were flushed, his eyes shone behind his rimless spectacles, and instead of carefully removing his rubbers and neatly placing them on the strip of mat laid for that purpose in a corner of the hallway, he pulled them off with reckless haste and tossed them aside. Then, still wearing his hat and overcoat, he undid the wrappings of the package he had brought with him and displayed a small, flat, leather case. When he opened the case Louise saw a bed of shabby green velvet in which rested the austere black and white forms of a set of chessmen.

'Aren't they beautiful?' George said. He ran a finger lovingly over one of the pieces. 'Look at the work on this: nothing fancy to stick away in a glass case, you understand, but everything neat and clean and ready for action the way it ought to be. All genuine ivory and ebony, and all handmade, every one of them.'

Louise's eyes narrowed. 'And just how much did you pay out for this stuff?'

'I didn't,' George said. 'That is, I didn't buy it. Mr Oelrichs gave it to me.'

'Oelrichs?' said Louise. 'You mean that old crank you brought home to dinner that time? The one who just sat and watched us like the cat that ate the canary, and wouldn't say a word unless you poked it out of him?'

'Oh, Louise!'

'Don't you "Oh, Louise" me! I thought I made my feelings about him mighty clear to you long before this. And, may I ask, why should our fine Mr Oelrichs suddenly decide to give you this thing?'

'Well,' George said uneasily, 'you know he's been pretty sick, and what with him needing only a few months more for retirement I was carrying most of his work for him. Today was his last day, and he gave me this as a kind of thank-you present. Said it was his favourite set, too, but he wanted to give me the best thing he could, and this was it.'

'How generous of Mr Oelrichs,' Louise remarked frigidly. 'Did it ever occur to him that if he wanted to pay you back for your time and trouble, something practical would be a lot more to the point?'

'Why, I was just doing him a favour, Louise. Even if he did offer me money or anything like that, I wouldn't take it.'

'The more fool you,' Louise sniffed. 'All right, take off your things, put them away right, and get ready for supper. It's just about ready.'

She moved toward the kitchen, and George trailed after her placatingly. 'You know, Louise, Mr Oelrichs said something that was very interesting.'

'I'm sure he did.'

'Well, he said there were some people in the world who *needed* chess – that when they learned to play it real well they'd see for themselves how much they needed it. And what I thought was that there's no reason why you and I ...'

She stopped short and faced him with her hands on her hips. 'You mean that after I'm done taking care of the house, and shopping, and cooking your hot meals, and mending and darning, then I'm supposed to sit down and learn how to play games with you! For a man going on fifty, George Huneker, you get some peculiar ideas.'

Pulling off his overcoat in the hallway, he reflected that there was small chance of his losing track of his age, at least not as long as Louise doted so much on reminding him. He had first heard about it a few months after his marriage when he was going on thirty and had been offered a chance to go into business for himself. He had heard about it every year since, on some occasion or other, although as he learned more and more about Louise he had fallen into fewer traps.

The only trouble was that Louise always managed to stay one jump ahead of him, and while in time he came to understand that she would naturally put her foot down at such things as his leaving a good steady job, or at their having a baby when times were hard (and in Louise's opinion they always were), or at buying the house outright when they could rent it so cheap, it still came as a surprise she so bitterly opposed the idea of having company to the house, or of reading some book he had just enjoyed, or of tuning in the radio to a symphony, or, as in this case, of taking up chess.

Company, she made it clear, was a bother and expense, small print hurt her eyes, symphonies gave her a splitting headache, and chess, it seemed, was something for which she could not possibly find time. Before they had been married, George thought unhappily, it had all been different somehow. They were always in the midst of a crowd of his friends, and when books or music or anything like that were the topics of discussion, she followed the talk with bright and vivacious interest. Now she just wanted to sit with her knitting every night while she listened to comedians bellowing over the radio.

Not being well, of course, could be one reason for all this. She suffered from a host of aches and pains which she dwelt on in such vivid detail at times that George himself could feel sympathetic twinges go through him. Their medicine chest bulged with remedies, their diet had dwindled to a bland and tasteless series of concoctions, and it was a rare month which did not find Louise running up a sizeable doctor's bill for the treatment of what George vaguely came to think of as 'women's troubles'.

Still, George would have been the first to point out that despite the handicaps she worked under, Louise had been as good a wife as a man could ask for. His salary over the years had hardly been luxurious, but penny by penny she had managed to put aside fifteen thousand dollars in their bank account. This was a fact known only to the two of them since Louise made it a point to dwell on their relative poverty in her conversations with anyone, and while George always felt some embarrassment when she did this, Louise pointed out that one of the best ways to save your money was not to let the world at large know you had any, and since a penny saved was a penny earned she was contributing as much to their income in her way as George was in his. This, while not reducing George's embarrassment, did succeed in glossing it with increased respect for Louise's wisdom and capability.

And when added to this was the knowledge that his home was always neat as a pin, his clothing carefully mended, and his health fanatically ministered to, it was easy to see why George chose to count his blessings rather than make an issue of anything so trivial as his wife's becoming his partner at chess. Which, as George himself might have admitted had you pinned him down to it, was a bit of a sacrifice, for in no time at all after receiving the set of chessmen he found himself a passionate devotee of the game. And chess, as he sometimes reflected while poring over his board of an evening with the radio booming in his ears and his wife's knitting needles flickering away contentedly, would seem to be a game greatly enhanced by the presence of an opponent. He did not reflect this ironically; there was no irony in George's nature.

Mr Oelrichs, in giving him the set, had said he would be available for instruction at any time. But since Louise had already indicated that that gentleman would hardly be a welcome guest in her home, and since she had often expressed decided opinions on any man who would leave his hearth and home to go traipsing about for no reason, George did not even think the matter worth broaching. Instead, he turned to a little text aptly entitled *An Invitation to Chess*, was led by the invitation to essay other and more difficult texts, and was thence led to a whole world of literature on chess, staggering in its magnitude and complexity.

He ate chess, drank chess, and slept chess. He studied the masters and past masters until he could quote chapter and verse from even their minor triumphs. He learned the openings, the middle game, and the end game. He learned to eschew the reckless foray which led nowhere in favour of the positional game where cunning strategy turned a side into a relentless force that inevitably broke and crushed the enemy before it. Strange names danced across his horizon: Alekhine, Capablanca, Lasker, Nimzovich, and he pursued them, drunk with the joy of discovery, through the ebony and ivory mazes of their universe.

But in all this there was still that one thing lacking: an opponent, a flesh-and-blood opponent against whom he could test himself. It was one thing, he sometimes thought disconsolately, to have a book at one's elbow while pondering a move; it would be quite another to ponder even the identical move with a man waiting across the board to turn it to his own advantage and destroy you with it. It became a growing hunger, that desire to make a move and see a hand reach across the table to answer it; it became a curious obsession so that at times, when Louise's shadow moved abruptly against the wall or a log settled in the fireplace, George would look up suddenly, half expecting to see the man seated in the empty chair opposite him.

He came to visualize the man quite clearly after a while. A quiet contemplative man much like himself, in fact, with greying hair and rimless spectacles that tended to slide a bit when he bent over the board. A man who played just a shade better than himself; not so well that he could not be beaten, but well enough to force George to his utmost to gain an occasional victory.

And there was one thing more he expected of this man: something a trifle unorthodox, perhaps, if one was a stickler for chess ritual. The man must prefer to play the white side all the time. It was the white side that moved first, that took the offensive until, perhaps, the tide could be turned against it. George himself infinitely preferred the black side, preferred to parry the thrusts and advances of white while he slowly built up a solid wall of defence against its climactic moves. *That* was the way to learn the game, George told himself; after a player learned how to make himself invulnerable on the defence, there was nothing he couldn't do on attack.

However, to practise one's defence still required a hand to set the offence in motion, and eventually George struck on a solution which, he felt with mild pride, was rather ingenious. He would set up the board, seat himself behind the black side, and then make the opening move for white. This he would counter with a black piece, after which he would move again for white, and so on until some decision was reached.

It was not long before the flaws in this system became distressingly obvious. Since he naturally favoured the black side, and since he knew both plans of battle from their inception, black won game after game with ridiculous ease. And after the twen-

tieth fiasco of this sort George sank back into his chair despairingly. If he could only put one side out of his mind completely
while he was moving for the other, why, there would be no
problem at all! Which, he realized cheerlessly, was a prospect
about as logical as an ancient notion he had come across in his
reading somewhere, the notion that if you cut a serpent in half,
the separated halves would then turn on each other and fight
themselves savagely to death.

He set up the board again after this glum reflection, and then
walked around the table and seated himself in white's chair. Now,
if he were playing the white side what would he do? A game depends not only on one's skill, he told himself, but also on one's
knowledge of his opponent. And not only on the opponent's
style of play, but also on his character, his personality, his whole
nature. George solemnly looked across the table at black's now
empty chair and brooded on this. Then slowly, deliberately, he
made his opening move.

After that, he quickly walked around the table and sat down
on black's side. The going, he found, was much easier here, and
almost mechanically he answered white's move. With a thrill of
excitement chasing inside him, he left his seat and moved around
to the other side of the board again, already straining hard to
put black and its affairs far out of his mind.

'For pity's sake, George, what *are* you doing?'

George started, and looked around dazedly. Louise was watching him, her lips compressed, her knitting dropped on her lap,
and her manner charged with such disapproval that the whole
room seemed to frown at him. He opened his mouth to explain,
and hastily thought better of it.

'Why, nothing,' he said, 'nothing at all.'

'Nothing at all!' Louise declared tartly. 'The way you're
tramping around, somebody would think you can't find a comfortable chair in the house. You know I ...'

Then her voice trailed off, her eyes became glassy, her body
straightened and became rigid with devouring attention. The
comedian on the radio had answered an insult with another evidently so devastating that the audience in the studio could do no
more than roar in helpless laughter. Even Louise's lips turned up

ever so slightly at the corners as she reached for her knitting again, and George gratefully seized this opportunity to drop into the chair behind black's side.

He had been on the verge of a great discovery, he knew that; but what exactly had it been? Was it that changing places physically had allowed him to project himself into the forms of two players, each separate and distinct from the other? If so, he was at the end of the line, George knew, because he would never be able to explain all that getting up and moving around to Louise.

But suppose the board itself were turned around after each move? Or, and George found himself charged with a growing excitement, since chess was completely a business of the mind anyhow – since, when one had mastered the game sufficiently it wasn't even necessary to use a board at all – wasn't the secret simply a matter of *turning oneself into the other player* when his move came?

It was white's move now, and George bent to his task. He was playing white's side, he must do what white would do – more than that, he must feel white's very emotions – but the harder he struggled and strained in his concentration, the more elusive became his goal. Again and again, at the instant he was about to reach his hand out, the thought of what black intended to do, of what black was surely *going* to do, slipped through his mind like a dot of quicksilver and made him writhe inwardly with a maddening sense of defeat.

This now became the obsession, and evening after evening he exercised himself at it. He lost weight, his face drew into haggard lines so that Louise was always at his heels during mealtimes trying to make him take an interest in her wholly uninteresting recipes. His interest in his job dwindled until it was barely perfunctory, and his superior, who at first had evinced no more than a mild suprise and irritation, started to shake his head ominously.

But with every game, every move, every effort he made, George felt with exultation he was coming nearer that goal. There would come a moment, he told himself with furious certainty, when he could view the side across the board with objectivity, with disinterest, with no more knowledge of its intentions and plans than he would have of any flesh-and-blood player who sat there; and when that day came, he would have achieved a triumph no other player before him could ever claim!

He was so sure of himself, so confident that the triumph lay beyond the next move each time he made a move, that when it came at last his immediate feeling was no more than a comfortable gratification and an expansive easing of all his nerves. Something like the feeling, he thought pleasurably, that a man gets after a hard day's work when he sinks into bed at night. Exactly that sort of feeling, in fact.

He had left the black position on the board perilously exposed through a bit of carelessness, and then in an effort to recover himself had moved the king's bishop in a neat defensive gesture that could cost white dear. When he looked up to study white's possible answer he saw White sitting there in the chair across the table, his fingertips gently touching each other, an ironic smile on his lips.

'Good,' said White pleasantly. 'Surprisingly good for you, George.'

At this, George's sense of gratification vanished like a soap bubble flicked by a casual finger. It was not only the amiable insult conveyed by the words which nettled him; equally disturbing was the fact that White was utterly unlike the man that George had been prepared for. He had not expected White to resemble him as one twin resembles another, yet feature for feature the resemblance was so marked that White could have been the image that stared back at him from his shaving mirror each morning. An image, however, which, unlike George's, seemed invested with a power and arrogance that was quite overwhelming. Here, George felt with a touch of resentment, was no man to hunch over a desk computing dreary rows of figures, but one who with dash and brilliance made great decisions at the head of a long committee table. A man who thought a little of tomorrow, but much more of today and the good things it offered. And one who would always find the price for those good things.

That much was evident in the matchless cut of White's clothing, in the grace and strength of the lean, well-manicured hands, in the merciless yet merry glint in the eyes that looked back into George's. It was when he looked into those eyes that George found himself fumbling for some thought that seemed to lie just beyond him. The image of himself was reflected so clearly in those eyes; perhaps it was not an image. Perhaps ...

He was jarred from his train of thought by White's moving a piece. 'Your move,' said White carelessly, 'that is, if you want to continue the game.'

George looked at the board and found his position still secure. 'Why shouldn't I want to continue the game? Our positions ...'

'For the moment are equal,' White interposed promptly. 'What you fail to consider is the long view: I am playing to win; you are playing only to keep from losing.'

'It seems very much the same thing,' argued George.

'But it is not,' said White, 'and the proof of that lies in the fact that I shall win this game, and every other game we ever play.'

The effrontery of this staggered George. 'Maroczy was a master who relied a good deal on defensive strategy,' he protested, 'and if you are familiar with his games ...'

'I am exactly as well acquainted with Maroczy's games as you are,' White observed, 'and I do not hesitate to say that had we ever played, I should have beaten him every game as well.'

George reddened. 'You think very well of yourself, don't you,' he said, and was surprised to see that instead of taking offence White was regarding him with a look of infinite pity.

'No,' White said at last, 'it is you who think well of me,' and then as if he had just managed to see and avoid a neatly baited trap, he shook his head and drew his lips into a faintly sardonic grimace. 'Your move,' he said.

With an effort George put aside the vaguely troubling thoughts that clustered in his mind, and made the move. He made only a few after that when he saw clearly that he was hopelessly and ignominiously beaten. He was beaten a second game, and then another after that, and then in the fourth game, he made a despairing effort to change his tactics. On his eleventh move he saw a devastating opportunity to go on the offensive, hesitated, refused it, and was lost again. At that George grimly set about placing the pieces back in their case.

'You'll be back tomorrow?' he said, thoroughly put out at White's obvious amusement.

'If nothing prevents me.'

George suddenly felt cold with fear. 'What could prevent you?' he managed to say.

White picked up the white queen and revolved it slowly between his fingers. 'Louise, perhaps. What if she decided not to let you indulge yourself in this fashion?'

'But why? Why should she? She's never minded up to now!'

'Louise, my good man, is an extremely stupid and petulant woman. ...'

'Now, that's uncalled for!' George said, stung to the quick.

'And,' White continued as if he had not been interrupted at all, 'she is the master here. Such people now and then like to affirm their mastery seemingly for no reason at all. Actually, such gestures are a sop to their vanity – as necessary to them as the air they breathe.'

George mustered up all the courage and indignation at his command. 'If those are your honest opinions,' he said bravely, 'I don't think you have the right to come to this house ever again.'

On the heels of his words Louise stirred in her armchair and turned toward him. 'George,' she said briskly, 'that's quite enough of that game for the evening. Don't you have anything better to do with your time?'

'I'm putting everything away now,' George answered hastily, but when he reached for the chessman still gripped between his opponent's fingers, he saw White studying Louise with a look that made him quail. White turned to him then, and his eyes were like pieces of dark glass through which one can see the almost unbearable light of a searing flame.

'Yes,' White said slowly. 'For what she is and what she has done to you I hate her with a consuming hate. Knowing that, do you wish me to return?'

The eyes were not unkind when they looked at him now, George saw, and the feel of the chessman which White thrust into his hand was warm and reassuring. He hesitated, cleared his throat, then, 'I'll see you tomorrow,' he said at last.

White's lips drew into that familiar sardonic grimace.

'Tomorrow, the next day, any time you want me,' he said. 'But it will always be the same. You will never beat me.'

Time proved that White had not underestimated himself. And time itself, as George learned, was something far better measured by an infinite series of chess games, by the moves within a chess game, than by any such device as a calendar or clock. The discovery was a delightful one; even more delightful was the realization that the world around him, when viewed clearly, had come to resemble nothing so much as an object seen through the wrong end of a binocular. All those people who pushed and prodded and poked and demanded countless explanations and apologies could be seen as sharp and clear as ever but nicely reduced in perspective, so that it was obvious that no matter how close they came, they could never really touch one.

There was a single exception to this: Louise. Every evening the world would close in around the chessboard and the figure of White lounging in the chair on the other side of it. But in a corner of the room sat Louise over her knitting, and the air around her was charged with a mounting resentment which would now and then eddy around George in the form of querulous complaints and demands from which there was no escape.

'How *can* you spend every minute at that idiotic game!' she demanded. 'Don't you have anything to talk to me about?' And, in fact, he did not, any more than he had since the very first years of his marriage when he had been taught that he had neither voice nor vote in running his home, that she did not care to hear about the people he worked with in his office, and that he could best keep to himself any reflections he had on some subject which was, by her own word, Highbrow.

'And how right she is,' White had once taken pains to explain derisively. 'If *you* had furnished your home it would be uncluttered and graceful, and Louise would feel awkward and out of place in it. If she comes to know the people you work with too well, she might have to befriend them, entertain them, set her blatant ignorance before them for judgement. No, far better under the circumstances that she dwells in her vacuum, away from unhappy judgements.'

As it always could, White's manner drove George to furious

resentment. 'For a set of opinions pulled out of a cocked hat that sounds very plausible,' he burst out. 'Tell me, how do you happen to know so much about Louise?'

White looked at him through veiled eyes. 'I know only what you know,' he said. 'No more and no less.'

Such passages left George sore and wounded, but for the sake of the game he endured them. When Louise was silent all the world retreated into unreality. Then the reality was the chessboard with White's hand hovering over it, mounting the attack, sweeping everything before it with a reckless brilliance that could only leave George admiring and dismayed.

In fact, if White had any weaknesses, George reflected mournfully, it was certainly not in his game, but rather in his deft and unpleasant way of turning each game into the occasion for a little discourse on the science of chess, a discourse which always wound up with some remarkably perverse and impudent reflections on George's personal affairs.

'You know that the way a man plays chess demonstrates that man's whole nature,' White once remarked. 'Knowing this, does it not strike you as significant that you always choose to play the defensive – and always lose?'

That sort of thing was bad enough, but White was at his most savage those times when Louise would intrude in a game: make some demand on George, or openly insist that he put away the board. Then White's jaw would set, and his eyes would flare with that terrible hate that always seemed to be smouldering in them when he regarded the woman.

Once when Louise had gone so far as to actually pick up a piece from the board and bang it back into the case, White came to his feet so swiftly and menacingly that George leaped up to forestall some rash action. Louise glared at him for that.

'You don't have to jump like that,' she snapped. 'I didn't break anything. But I can tell you, George Huneker: if you don't stop this nonsense I'll do it for you. I'll break every one of these things to bits if that's what it takes to make you act like a human being again!'

'Answer her!' said White. 'Go ahead, why don't you answer her!' And caught between these two fires George could do no more than stand there and shake his head helplessly.

It was this episode, however, which marked a new turn in White's manner: the entrance of a sinister purposefulness thinly concealed in each word and phrase.

'If she knew how to play the game,' he said, 'she might respect it, and you would have nothing to fear.'

'It so happens,' George replied defensively, 'that Louise is too busy for chess.'

White turned in his chair to look at her and then turned back with a grim smile. 'She is knitting. And, it seems to me, she is always knitting. Would you call that being busy?'

'Wouldn't you?'

'No,' said White, 'I wouldn't. Penelope spent her years at the loom to keep off importunate suitors until her husband returned. Louise spends her years at knitting to keep off life until death comes. She takes no joy in what she does; one can see that with half an eye. But each stitch dropping off the end of those needles brings her one instant nearer death, and, although she does not know it, she rejoices in it.'

'And you make all that out of the mere fact that she won't play chess?' cried George incredulously.

'Not alone chess,' said White. 'Life.'

'And what do you mean by that word *life*, the way you use it?'

'Many things,' said White. 'The hunger to learn, the desire to create, the ability to feel vast emotions. Oh, many things.'

'Many things, indeed,' George scoffed. 'Big words, that's all they are.' But White only drew his lips into that sardonic grimace and said, 'Very big. Far too big for Louise, I'm afraid,' and then by moving a piece forced George to redirect his attention to the board.

It was as if White had discovered George's weak spot and took a sadistic pleasure in returning to probe it again and again. And he played his conversational gambits as he made his moves at chess: cruelly, unerringly, always moving forward to the inescapable conclusion with a sort of flashing audacity. There were times when George, writhing helplessly, thought of asking him to drop the subject of Louise once and for all, but he could never bring himself to do so. Something in the recesses of George's mind warned him that these conventional fancies were as much a part of White as his capacity for chess, and that if George wanted him at all it would have to be on his own terms.

And George did want him, wanted him desperately, the more so on such an evening as that dreadful one when he came home to tell Louise that he would not be returning to his office for a while. He had not been discharged, of course, but there had been something about his taking a rest until he felt in shape again. Although, he hastily added in alarm as he saw Louise's face go slack and pale, he never felt better in his life.

In the scene that followed, with Louise standing before him and passionately telling him things about himself that left him sick and shaken, he found White's words pouring through his mind in a bitter torment. It was only when Louise was sitting exhausted in her armchair, her eyes fixed blankly on the wall before her, her knitting in her lap to console her, and he was at his table setting up the pieces, that he could feel the brackish tide of his pain receding.

'And yet there is a solution for all this,' White said softly, and turned his eyes toward Louise. 'A remarkably simple solution when one comes to think of it.'

George felt a chill run through him. 'I don't care to hear about it,' he said hoarsely.

'Have you ever noticed, George,' White persisted, 'that that piddling, hackneyed picture on the wall, set in that baroque monstrosity of a frame that Louise admires so much, is exactly like a pathetic little fife trying to make itself heard over an orchestra that is playing its loudest?'

George indicated the chessboard. 'You have the first move,' he said.

'Oh, the game,' White said. 'The game can wait, George. For the moment I'd much prefer to think what this room – the whole fine house, in fact – could be if it were all yours, George. Yours alone.'

'I'd rather get on with the game,' George pleaded.

'There's another thing, George,' White said slowly, and when he leaned forward George saw his own image again staring at him strangely from those eyes, 'another fine thing to think of. If you were all alone in this room, in this house, why, there wouldn't be anyone to tell you when to stop playing chess. You could play morning, noon, and night, and all around to the next morning if you cared to!

'And that's not all, George. You can throw that picture out of the window and hang something respectable on the wall: a few good prints, perhaps – nothing extravagant, mind you – but a few good ones that stir you a bit the first time you come into the room each day and see them.

'And recordings! I understand they're doing marvellous things with recordings today, George. Think of a whole room filled with them: opera, symphony, concerto, quartet – just take your pick and play them to your heart's content!'

The sight of his image in those eyes always coming nearer, the jubilant flow of words, the terrible meaning of those words set George's head reeling. He clapped his hands over his ears and shook his head frantically.

'You're mad!' he cried. 'Stop it!' And then he discovered to his horror that even with his hands covering his ears he could hear White's voice as clearly and distinctly as ever.

'Is it the loneliness you're afraid of, George? But that's foolish. There are so many people who would be glad to be your friends, to talk to you, and, what's better, to listen to you. There are some who would even love you, if you chose.'

'Loneliness?' George said unbelievingly. 'Do you think it's loneliness I'm afraid of?'

'Then what is it?'

'You know as well as I,' George said in a shaking voice, 'what you're trying to lead me to. How could you expect me, expect any decent man, to be that cruel!'

White bared his teeth disdainfully. 'Can you tell me anything more cruel than a weak and stupid woman whose only ambition in life was to marry a man infinitely superior to her and then cut him down to her level so that her weakness and stupidity could always be concealed?'

'You've got no right to talk about Louise like that!'

'I have every right,' said White grimly, and somehow George knew in his heart that this was the dreadful truth. With a rising panic he clutched the edge of the table.

'I won't do it!' he said distractedly. 'I'll never do it, do you understand!'

'But it will be done!' White said, and his voice was so naked with terrible decision that George looked up to see Louise coming toward the table with her sharp little footsteps. She stood over it, her mouth working angrily, and then through the confusion of his thoughts he heard her voice echoing the same words again and again. 'You fool!' she was saying wildly. 'It's this chess! I've had enough of it!' And suddenly she swept her hand over the board and dashed the pieces from it.

'No!' cried George, not at Louise's gesture, but at the sight of White standing before her, the heavy poker raised in his hand. 'No!' George shouted again, and started up to block the fall of the poker, but knew even as he did so that it was too late.

Louise might have been dismayed at the untidy way her remains were deposited in the official basket; she would certainly have cried aloud (had she been in a condition to do so) at the unsightly scar on the polished woodwork made by the basket as it was dragged along the floor and borne out of the front door. Inspector Lund, however, merely closed the door casually behind the little cortege and turned back to the living room.

Obviously the Lieutenant had completed his interview of the quiet little man seated in the chair next to the chess table, and obviously the Lieutenant was not happy. He paced the centre of the floor, studying his notes with a furrowed brow, while the little man watched him, silent and motionless.

'Well?' said Inspector Lund.

'Well,' said the Lieutenant, 'there's just one thing that doesn't tie in. From what I put together, here's a guy who's living his life all right, getting along fine, and all of a sudden he finds he's got another self, another personality. He's like a man split in two parts, you might say.'

'Schizoid,' remarked Inspector Lund. 'That's not unusual.'

'Maybe not,' said the Lieutenant. 'Anyhow, this other self is no good at all, and sure enough it winds up doing this killing.'

'That all seems to tie in,' said Inspector Lund. 'What's the hitch?'

'Just one thing,' the Lieutenant stated: 'a matter of identity.' He frowned at his notebook, and then turned to the little man in the chair next to the chess table. 'What did you say your name was?' he demanded.

The little man drew his lips into a faintly sardonic grimace of rebuke. 'Why, I've told you that so many times before, Lieutenant, surely you couldn't have forgotten it again.' The little man smiled pleasantly.

'My name is White.'

The Best of Everything

In Arthur's eyes they were all seemingly cut from one pattern. They were uniformly tall and well-built. They had regular features set into nicely tanned faces and capped by crew cuts. Their clothing was expensively staid; their manners were impeccable. They came from impressive Families and impressive Schools, and they regarded these things casually. Among the bees that swarmed through the midtown hive, through Gothic piles redolent with the pleasant scent of gilt-edged securities, through glass pinnacles like futuristic fish bowls, they were not the most obtrusive, yet they were not lost.

To their jobs they brought the qualifications of Family and School and the capacity for looking politely eager when a superior addressed them. Actually, they as casual about their jobs as they were about everything else, because they were cushioned with money. And for all this Arthur hated them, and would have sold his soul to be one of them.

Physically he might have passed muster. He was a tall, extremely good-looking young man – when he walked by, few women could resist giving him that quick little sidelong glance which means they are interested, even if unavailable – and he had a sober poise which was largely the product of shrewd observation and good self-control. But he came from no impressive Family, no impressive School – and he had no money outside of his moderate salary. His parents were dead (their legacy had barely paid their funeral expenses), he had left high school before graduation to go to work, and uneasily shifted jobs until he had recently come to port in Horton & Son, and he could, at any moment he was asked, have stated his net worth to the penny: the total of bank account, wallet, and change pocket. Obviously, he could not afford to be casual, as a fine young man should.

That phrase, *fine young man*, crystallized his hatred of the type. He had been standing outside Mr Horton's door one morning when the two sons of a client had been ushered out. Their eyes flicked over Arthur in the fraction of a second, instantly marked that he was not one of them, and turned blankly indifferent. Nothing was said, nothing done, but he was put neatly in his place in that moment and left to stand there with the hate and anger boiling in him. And he couldn't hit back, that was the worst of it; there was no way of touching them. Their homes, their clubs, their lives were inaccessible.

When the elevator door closed behind them Mr Horton seemed to notice Arthur for the first time. 'Fine young men,' he observed, almost wistfully, gesturing toward the elevator door, and the phrase had been planted. Not only planted, but fertilized on the spot by Mr Horton's tone which, to Arthur's inflamed mind, appeared to add: *They belong to my world, but you do not.*

And to make it worse, of course, there was Ann. Ann Horton.

It is the traditional right of every enterprising young man to apply himself as diligently to romance as to business, and to combine the highest degree of success in both by marrying the boss's daughter. And if the daughter happened to be as beautiful and desirable, and, to use the admiring expression of those who knew her, unspoiled, as Ann Horton, so much the better.

But what Arthur knew instinctively was that there are different degrees of being unspoiled. Thus, if a girl who desperately yearns for a forty-foot cabin cruiser and finally settles for a twenty-foot speedboat is unspoiled, Ann Horton was unspoiled. It is not quite sufficient to approach someone like this bringing only a burning passion and an eagerness to slay dragons. It is also necessary to come riding in golden armour, mounted on a blooded horse, and bearing orchestra seats to the best musical comedy in town. And, if the suitor is to make his point explicit, not on rare occasions, but frequently.

All this and more Arthur brooded over as he lay on his bed in Mrs Marsh's rooming house night after night and studied the ceiling. His thoughts were maddening, whirling around on themselves like the apocryphal snake seizing its own tail and then devouring itself. Ann Horton had looked at him more than once the way all women looked at him. If he could only meet her, offer her the image of himself that she required, was marriage out of the question? But to meet her on terms took money, and, ironically, the only chance he ever had of getting money was to marry her! Good Lord, he thought, if he ever could do that he'd have enough money to throw into the face of every fine young man he'd ever hated.

So the thoughts slowly reshaped themselves, and without his quite knowing it Ann Horton became the means, not the end. The end would be the glory that comes to those who, without counting their money, can afford the best of everything. *The best of everything*, Arthur would say dreamily to himself, and his eyes would see beautiful, expensive pictures like clouds moving across the ceiling.

Charlie Prince was a young man who obviously had known the best of everything. He made his entrance into Arthur's life one lunch hour as Arthur sat finishing his coffee, his eyes on a Horton & Son prospectus spread on the table before him, his thoughts in a twenty-foot speedboat with Ann Horton.

'Hope you don't mind my asking,' said Charlie Prince, 'but do you work for old Horton?'

The voice was the voice of someone from a Family and a School; even the use of the word 'old' was a natural part of it, since the word was now in vogue among *them*, and could be applied to anything, no matter what its age might be. Arthur looked up from shoes, to suit, to shirt, to necktie, to hat, his mind mechanically tabbing them *Oliver Moore, Brooks, Sulka, Bronzini, Cavanaugh,* and then stopped short at the face. True, it was tanned, marked by regular features, and capped by the inevitable crew haircut, but there was something else about it. Some small lines about the eyes, some twist of the lips ...

'That's right,' Arthur said warily, 'I work for Horton's.'

'Is it all right if I sit down here? My name's Charlie Prince.'

It turned out that Charlie Prince had seen the prospectus on the table, had once worked for Horton's himself, and couldn't resist stopping to ask how the old place was coming along.

'All right, I guess,' said Arthur, and then remarked, 'I don't remember seeing you around.'

'Oh, that was before your time, I suppose, and I'm sure the office is hardly encouraged to talk about me. You see, I'm sort of a blot on its escutcheon. I left under rather a cloud, if you get what I mean.'

'Oh,' said Arthur, and felt a quick, bitter envy for anyone who could afford to be incompetent, insubordinate even, and could leave a firm like Horton's so casually.

Charlie Prince, it appeared, read his thoughts quite accurately. 'No,' he said, 'it doesn't have anything to do with my not being able to hold down the job, if that's what you're thinking. It was a bit of dishonesty, really. Some cheques I forged – stuff like that.'

Arthur's jaw dropped.

'I know,' observed Charlie Prince cheerfully. 'You figure that when someone gets caught in a business like that he ought to be all tears and remorse, all sackcloth and ashes, and such. But I'm not. Oh, of course, I was all remorse at getting caught by that idiot, meddling accountant, but you can hardly blame me for that.'

'But why did you do it?'

Charlie Prince frowned. 'I don't look like one of those silly psychopaths who just steals to get a thrill from it, do I? It was for money, of course. It's always for money.'

'Always?'

'Oh, I worked in other places besides Horton's and I was always leaving under a cloud. Matter of fact, it wasn't until I was in Horton's that I learned the biggest lesson of my life.' He leaned forward and tapped his forefinger on the table significantly. 'That business of tracing someone's signature is the bunk. Absolute bunk. If you're going to forge a name you just have to practise writing it freehand, and keep on practising until you can set it down slapdash, like that. It's the only way.'

'But you got caught there, too.'

'That was carelessness. I was cashing the cheques, but I didn't bother to make entries about them in the books. And you know what an accountant can be if his books don't balance.'

Arthur found himself fascinated, but also found himself unable to frame the question he wanted to ask and yet remain within the bounds of politeness. 'Then what happened? Did they – did you ...?'

'You mean, arrested, sent to jail, stuff like that?' Charlie Prince looked at Arthur pityingly. 'Of course not. You know how those companies are about publicity like that, and when my father made the money good that's all there was to it.'

'And nothing at all happened to you?' Arthur said, awestruck.

'Well,' Charlie Prince admitted, 'something *had* to happen, of course, especially after that last performance when my father boiled up like an old steam kettle about it. But it wasn't too bad, really. It was just that I became a sort of local remittance man.'

'A what?' said Arthur blankly.

'A sort of local remittance man. You know how those old families in England would ship their black-sheep offspring off to Australia or somewhere just to keep them off the scene, then send them an allowance and tell them it would show up regularly as long as sonny stayed out of sight? Well, that's what happened to me. At first the old man was just going to heave me out into the cold and darkness without even a penny, but the women in my family have soft hearts, and he was convinced otherwise. I would get a monthly allowance – about half of what I needed to live on, as it turned out – but for the rest of my life I had to steer clear of the family and its whole circle. And I can tell you, it's a mighty big circle.'

'Then you're not supposed to be in New York, are you?'

'I said I was a local remittance man. Meaning, I can be anywhere I please as long as I am not heard or seen by any of my family or its three million acquaintances. In which case I merely drop a note to the family lawyer stating my address, and on the first of each month I receive my allowance.'

'Well,' said Arthur, 'considering everything, I'd say your father was being very decent about it.'

Charlie Prince sighed. 'Truth to tell, he's not a bad old sort at all. But he's cursed by a morbid yearning toward a certain kind of holy young prig which I am not. You know what I mean. The sort of young squirt who's all bland exterior, bland interior, and not a spark anywhere. If I had turned out like that, everything would have been just dandy. But I didn't. So here I am, a veritable Ishmael, two weeks before allowance comes due, locked out of his hotel room ...'

Arthur felt an inexplicable stirring of excitement. 'Locked out?'

'That's what happens when you can't pay your rent. It's a law or a code or something. Anyhow, it's damn thoughtless whatever it is, and what I'm leading up to is, in return for the story of my life, such as it is, you might see your way clear to making a loan. Not too small a one either; a sort of medium-sized loan. I'll guarantee to pay you back the first of the month and with fair interest.' Charlie Prince's voice now had an openly pleading note. 'I'll admit that I have my dishonest side, but I've never welshed on a debt in my whole life. Matter of fact,' he explained, 'the only reason I got myself into trouble was because I was so anxious to pay my debts.'

Arthur looked at Charlie Prince's perfect clothes; he saw Charlie Prince's easy poise; he heard Charlie Prince's well-modulated voice sounding pleasantly in his ears, and the stirring of excitement suddenly took meaning.

'Look,' he said, 'where do you live now?'

'Nowhere, of course, not as long as I'm locked out. But I'll meet you here the first of the month on the minute. I can swear you don't have to worry about getting the money back. The way I've been talking about things ought to prove I'm on the dead level with you.'

'I don't mean that,' said Arthur. 'I mean, would you want to share a room with me? If I lent you enough money to clear up your hotel bill and get your things out of there, would you move in with me? I've got a nice room; it's in an old house but very well kept. Mrs Marsh – that is, the landlady – is the talky kind and very fussy about things, but you can see she's the sort to keep a place nice. And it's very cheap; it would save you a lot of money.'

He stopped short then with the realization that this was turning into a vehement sales talk, and that Charlie Prince was regarding him quizzically.

'What is it?' said Charlie Prince. 'Are you broke, too?'

'No, it has nothing to do with money. I have the money to lend you, don't I?'

'Then why the fever to share the room? Especially with me, that is.'

Arthur took his courage in both hands. 'All right, I'll tell you. You have something I want.'

Charlie Prince blinked. 'I do?'

'Listen to me,' Arthur said. 'I never had any of the things you had, and it shows. Somehow, it shows. I know it does, because you wouldn't ever talk to any of those young men, the sort your father likes, the way you talk to me. But I don't care about that. What I care about is finding out exactly what makes you like that, what makes them all like that. It's some kind of polish that a good family and money can rub on you so that it never comes off. And that's what I want.'

Charlie Prince looked at him wonderingly. 'And you think that if we share a room some of this mysterious polish, this whatever-it-is, will rub off on you?'

'You let me worry about that,' said Arthur. He drew out his chequebook and a pen, and laid them on the table before him. 'Well?' he said.

Charlie Prince studied the chequebook thoughtfully. 'I'll admit I haven't any idea of what I'm selling,' he said, 'but it's a sale.'

As it turned out, they made excellent room-mates. There is no greater compatability than that between a good talker and a good listener, and since Charlie Prince liked nothing better than to pump amiably from a bottomless well of anecdote and reminiscence, and Arthur made an almost feverishly interested audience, life in the second-floor front at Mrs Marsh's rooming house was idyllic.

There were some very small flies in the ointment, of course. At times, Charlie Prince might have had cause to reflect that he had found *too* good a listener in Arthur, considering Arthur's insatiable appetite for detail. It can be quite disconcerting for a raconteur embarked on the story of a yachting experience to find that he must describe the dimensions of the yacht, its structure, its method of operation, and then enter into a lecture on the comparative merits of various small boats, before he can get to the point of the story itself. Or to draw full value from the narrative of an intriguing little episode concerning a young woman met in a certain restaurant, when one is also required to add footnotes on the subjects of what to say to a *maître d'hôtel*, how to order, how to tip, how to dress for every occasion, and so on, *ad infinitum*.

It might also have distressed Charlie Prince, who had commendable powers of observation, to note that Arthur was becoming subtly cast in his own image. The inflection of voice, the choice of words and their usage, the manner of sitting, walking, standing, the gestures of hands, the very shades of expression which Arthur came to adopt, all had the rather uncomfortable quality of showing Charlie Prince to himself in a living mirror.

For Arthur's part the one thing that really shocked him in his relationship was the discovery of the childishness of Charlie Prince and his small world. From all he could gather, Arthur decided sombrely, Charlie Prince and his like emerged from childhood into adolescence, and stopped short there. Physically, they might grow still larger and more impressive; but mentally and emotionally, they were all they would ever be. They would learn adult catchwords and mannerisms, but underneath? Of course, it was nothing that Arthur ever chose to mention aloud.

His feeling on the subject was heightened by the matter of Charlie Prince's allowance. On the first of each month Mrs Marsh would smilingly enter the room bearing an envelope addressed to Charlie Prince. It was an expensive-looking envelope, and if one held it up to the light reflectively, as Charlie Prince always did before opening it, it was possible to make out the outlines of an expensive-looking slip of paper. A cheque for five hundred dollars signed by James Llewellyn. 'The family's personal lawyer,' Charlie Prince had once explained, and added with some bitterness, 'It wasn't hard enough having one father like mine, so old Llewellyn's been playing second father since I was a kid.'

To Charlie Prince the amount was a pittance. To Arthur it was the Key. The Key to the enchanted garden just outside Arthur's reach; the Key to Bluebeard's chamber which you were forbidden to use; the Key to Ann Horton. It would not pay for what you wanted, but it would open the door.

Even more tantalizing to Arthur was the fact that for a few hours each month it was all his. Charlie would endorse it, and then Arthur would obligingly stop in at the bank where he had his own small account and cash it there. On his return he would carefully deduct the amount of Charlie Prince's share of the rent, the amount that Charlie Prince had borrowed from him the last week or two of the preceding month, and then turn the rest over to his room-mate. It was at Charlie Prince's insistence that he did this. 'If you want to make sure that I'm square with my rent and whatever I owe you,' he had explained, 'this is the best way. Besides, you can cash it easily, and I seem to have a lot of trouble that way.'

Thus, for a few hours each month Arthur was another man. Charlie Prince was generous about lending his wardrobe, and Arthur made it a point on cheque-cashing day especially to wear one of those wondrously cut and textured suits, which looked as if it had been tailored for him. And in the breast pocket of that suit was a wallet containing five hundred dollars in crisp new bills. It was no wonder that it happened to be one of those days on which he made the impression he had dreamed of making.

He entered his employer's office, and Ann Horton was seated on a corner of the desk there, talking to her father. She glanced at Arthur as he stood there, and then stopped short in what she was saying to look him up and down with open admiration.

'Well,' she said to her father, 'I've seen this young man here and there in the office several times. Don't you think it's about time you had the manners to introduce us?'

Her manner of address startled Arthur, who had somehow always visualized Mr Horton as a forbidding figure poised on a mountaintop fingering a thunderbolt. But it was even more startling when Mr Horton, after what seemed to be a moment of uncertain recognition, made the introduction in terms that sounded like music to Arthur's ears. Arthur, he said warmly, was a fine young man. It would be a pleasure to introduce him.

That was Arthur's golden opportunity – and he flubbed it. Flubbed it miserably. What he said was pointless; the way he said it made it sound even more mawkish and clumsy than seemed possible. And even while he was watching the glow fade from Ann Horton's face he knew what the trouble was, and cursed himself and the whole world for it.

The money wasn't *his*, that was the thing. If it were he could be seeing her that evening, and the next, and the one after that. But it wasn't. It was a meaningless bulge in his wallet that could take him this far, and no farther. And that knowledge made everything else meaningless: the clothes, the manner, everything he had made himself into. Without the money it was all nonsense. With it ...

With it! He had been looking merely ill at ease; now he looked physically ill under the impact of the thought that struck him. An instant concern showed in Ann Horton's lovely eyes. Apparently she was a girl with strong maternal instinct.

'You're not well,' she said.

The idea, the glorious realization, was a flame roaring through him now. He rose from it like a phoenix.

'No, I don't feel very well,' he answered, and could hardly recognize his own voice as he spoke, 'but it's nothing serious. Really, it isn't.'

'Well, you ought to go home right now,' she said firmly. 'I have the car downstairs, and it won't be any trouble at all ...'

Arthur mentally struck himself on the forehead with his fist. He had thrown away one opportunity; did he have to throw this one away as well? Yet, Mrs Marsh's rooming house had never appeared as wretched as it did just then; it was impossible to have her drive him there.

Inspiration put the words into his mouth, the proper words to impress father and daughter. 'There's so much work to be done,' said Arthur, wistfully courageous, 'that I can't possibly leave it.' And then he added with as much ease as if he had practised the lines for hours. 'But I do want to see you again. Do you think if I called tomorrow evening ...?'

After that, he told himself grimly whenever the fire inside him threatened to flicker uncertainly, he had no choice. And Charlie Prince, of course, was not even offered a choice. At exactly seven minutes before midnight, after considerable choked protest and thrashing around, Charlie Prince lay dead on his bed. Entirely dead, although Arthur's fingers remained clasped around his throat for another long minute just to make sure.

It has been remarked that the man with the likeliest chance of getting away with murder is the man who faces his victim in a crowd, fires a bullet into him, and then walks off – which is a way of saying that it is the devious and overly ingenious method of murder that will hang the murderer. To that extent Arthur had committed his murder wisely, although not out of any wisdom.

The fact is that from the moment he had left Ann Horton to the moment he finally released his fingers from Charlie Prince's throat he had lived in a sort of blind fever of knowing what had to be done without a thought of how it was to be done. And when at last he stood looking down at the body before him, with the full horror of what had happened bursting in his mind, he was at a complete loss. The soul had departed, no question about that. But the body remained, and what in the Lord's name was one to do with it?

He could bundle it into the closet, get it out of sight at least, but what would be the point of that? Mrs Marsh came in every morning to make up the room and empty the wastebaskets. Since there was no lock on the closet door there was no way of keeping her out of it.

Or take Charlie Prince's trunk standing there in the corner. He could deposit the body in it, and ship it somewhere. Ship it where? He put his mind to the question desperately, but was finally forced to the conclusion that there was no place in the world to which you could ship a trunk with a body in it, and rest assured that murder wouldn't out.

But he was on the right track with that trunk, and when the solution came at last, he recognized it instantly and eagerly. The storage room in Mrs Marsh's was a dank cavern in the depths of the house, barred by a heavy door, which, though never locked, made it a desolate and chilly place no matter what the season. Since there was no traffic in that room, a body could moulder there for years without anyone being the wiser. Eventually, it could be disposed of with no difficulty; the object now was to get it into the trunk and down to the storage room.

To Arthur's annoyance he discovered that even though the trunk was a large one it made a tight fit, and it was a messy business getting everything arranged neatly. But at last he had it bolted tightly, and out into the hallway. It was when he was midway down the stairs that the accident happened. He felt the trunk slipping down his back, gave it a violent heave to right it, and the next instant saw it go sliding over his head to crash down the rest of the distance to the floor with a thunder that shook the house. He was after it in an instant, saw that it remained firmly bolted, and then realized that he was standing eye to eye with Mrs Marsh.

She was poised there like a frightened apparition, clad in a white flannel nightgown that fell to her ankles, her fingers to her lips, her eyes wide.

'Dear me,' she said, 'dear me, you should be more careful!'

Arthur flung himself in front of the trunk as if she had vision that could penetrate its walls. 'I'm sorry,' he stammered; 'I'm terribly sorry. I didn't mean to make any noise, but somehow it slipped ...'

She shook her head with gentle severity. 'You might have scratched the walls. Or hurt yourself.'

'No,' he assured her hastily, 'there's no damage done. None.'

She peered around him at the trunk. 'Why, that's that nice Mr Prince's trunk, isn't it? Wherever can you be taking it at this hour?'

Arthur felt the perspiration start on his forehead. 'Nowhere,' he said hoarsely, and then when she knit her brows in wonder at this he quickly added, 'That is, to the storage room. You see, Charlie – Mr Prince – was supposed to give me a hand with it, but when he didn't show up I decided to try it myself.'

'But it must be so heavy.'

Her warmly sympathetic tone served nicely to steady his nerves. His thoughts started to move now with the smooth precision of the second hand on a good watch.

'I suppose it is,' he said, and laughed deprecatingly, 'but it seemed better to do it myself than keep waiting for Mr Prince to help. He's very unreliable, you know. Just takes off when he wants to, and you never know how long he'll be gone.'

'I think it's a shame,' said Mrs Marsh firmly.

'No, no, he's a bit eccentric, that's all. But really very nice when you get to know him.' Arthur took a grip on the trunk. 'I'll get it down the rest of the way easily enough,' he said.

A thought struck Mrs Marsh. 'Oh, dear me,' she chirped, 'perhaps everything did happen for the best. I mean, your making a noise and bringing me out and all. You see, there's a lock on the storage room now, and you'd never have got in. I'll just slip on a robe and take care of that.'

She went ahead of him down the creaking cellar steps, and waited in the storage room until he trundled the trunk into it. A dim light burned there, and, as he had remembered dust lay thick over everything in sight. Mrs Marsh shook her head over it.

'It's dreadful,' she said, 'but there's really no point in trying to do anything about it. Why, I don't believe anyone uses this room from one year to the next! The only reason I put the lock on the door was because the insurance company wanted it there.'

Arthur shifted from one foot to the other. His mission completed, he was willing, in fact, anxious, to leave, but Mrs Marsh seemed oblivious to this.

'I don't encourage transients,' she said. 'What I like is a nice steady gentleman boarder who's no fuss and bother. Now, take that trunk there,' she pointed a bony forefinger at what appeared to be a mound of ashes, but which proved on a second look to be a trunk buried under years of dust. 'When that gentleman moved in ...'

Arthur found himself swaying on his feet while the gentle chirping went on and on. In this fashion he learned about the gentleman in the first-floor rear, the gentleman in the second-floor rear, and the gentleman in the third-floor front. It was as though her conversational stream had been dammed up so long that now that it was released there was no containing it. And through it all he sustained himself with one thought. He had got away with murder – really and literally got away with murder. When the door to the storage room closed behind him, Charlie Prince could rot away without a soul in the world being the wiser. The cheques would come every month, five hundred dollars each and every month, and there was Ann Horton and the world of glory ahead. *The best of everything*, Arthur thought in and around Mrs Marsh's unwearying voice, and he knew then what it felt like to be an emperor incognito.

The monologue had to come to an end some time, and the heavy door was locked and stayed locked, and Arthur entered his new station with the confidence that is supposed to be the lot of the righteous, but which may also come to those who have got away with murder and know it beyond the shadow of a doubt. And even the tiniest fragment of unease could not possibly remain after he met Mrs Marsh in the hallway one evening a few weeks later.

'You were right,' she said, pursing her lips sympathetically. 'Mr Prince *is* eccentric, isn't he?'

'He is?' said Arthur uncertainly.

'Oh, yes. Likes practising writing his name on every piece of paper he can get his hands on. Just one sheet of paper after another with nothing on it but his name!'

Arthur abruptly remembered his wastebasket, and then thought with a glow of undeserved self-admiration, how everything, even unforgiveable carelessness, worked for him.

'I'm sure,' observed Mrs Marsh, 'that a grown man can find better things to do with his time than that. It just goes to show you.'

'Yes,' said Arthur, 'it certainly does.'

So, serenity reigned over Mrs Marsh's. It reigned elsewhere, too, since Arthur had no difficulty at all in properly endorsing those precious cheques, and even less trouble in spending the money. Using Charlie Prince's wardrobe as his starting point, he built his into a thing of quiet splendour. Drawing from Charlie Prince's narratives, he went to the places where one should be seen, and behaved as one should behave. His employer beamed on him with a kindly eye which became almost affectionate when Arthur mentioned the income a generous aunt had provided for him; his acquaintance with Ann Horton, who had seemed strangely drawn to him from the first evening they spent together, soon blossomed into romance.

He found Ann Horton everything he had ever imagined – passionate, charming, devoted. Of course, she had her queer little reticences, dark little places in her own background that she chose not to touch upon, but, as he reminded himself, who was he to cast stones? So he behaved himself flawlessly up to the point where they had to discuss the wedding, and then they had their first quarrel.

There was no question about the wedding itself. It was to take place in June, the month of brides; it was to be followed by a luxurious honeymoon; after which, Arthur would enter into a position of importance in the affairs of Horton & Son at a salary commensurate with that position, of course. No, there was no question about the wedding – the envy in the eyes of every fine young man who had ever courted Ann Horton attested to that – but there was a grave question about the ceremony.

'But *why* do you insist on a big ceremony?' she demanded. 'I think they're dreadful things. All those people and all that fuss. It's like a Roman circus.'

He couldn't explain to her, and that complicated matters. After all, there is no easy way of explaining to any girl that her wedding is not only to be a nuptial, but also a sweet measure of revenge. It would be all over the papers; the whole world of fine young men would be on hand to witness it. They had to be there, or it would be tasteless in the mouth.

'And why do you insist on a skimpy little private affair?' he asked in turn. 'I should think a girl's wedding would be the most important thing in the world to her. That she'd want to do it up proud. Standing there in the living room with your father and aunt doesn't seem like any ceremony at all.'

'But you'll be there, too,' she said. 'That's what makes it a ceremony.'

He was not to be put off by any such feminine wit, however, and he let her know it. In the end, she burst into tears and fled, leaving him as firm in his convictions as ever. If it cost him his neck, he told himself angrily, he was not going to have any hit-

and-run affair fobbed off on him as the real thing. He'd have the biggest cathedral in town, the most important people – the best of everything.

When they met again she was in a properly chastened mood, so he was properly magnanimous.

'Darling,' she said, 'did you think I was very foolish carrying on the way I did?'

'Of course not, Ann. Don't you think I understand how high-strung you are, and how seriously you take this?'

'You are a darling, Arthur,' she said, 'really you are. And perhaps, in a way, your insistence on a big ceremony has done more for us than you'll ever understand.'

'In what way?' he asked.

'I can't tell you that. But I can tell you that I haven't been as happy in years as I'm going to be if things work out.'

'What things?' he asked, completely at sea in the face of this feminine ambiguity.

'Before I can even talk about it there's one question you must answer, Arthur. And please, promise you'll answer truthfully.'

'Of course I will.'

'Then can you find it in your heart to forgive someone who's done a great wrong? Someone who's done wrong, but suffered for it?'

He grimaced inwardly. 'Of course I can. I don't care what wrong anyone's done. It's my nature to forgive him.'

He almost said *her* but caught himself in time. After all, if that was the way she wanted to build up to a maidenly confession, why spoil it? But there seemed to be no confession forthcoming. She said nothing more about the subject – instead, spent the rest of the evening in such a giddy discussion of plans and arrangements that by the time he left her the matter was entirely forgotten.

He was called into Mr Horton's office late the next afternoon, and when he entered the room he saw Ann there. From her expression and from her father's he could guess what they had been discussing, and he felt a pleasant triumph in that knowledge.

'Arthur,' said Mr Horton, 'please sit down.'

Arthur sat down, crossed his legs, and smiled at Ann.

'Arthur,' said Mr Horton, 'I have something serious to discuss with you.'

'Yes, sir,' said Arthur, and waited patiently for Mr Horton to finish arranging three pencils, a pen, a letter opener, a memorandum pad, and a telephone before him on the desk.

'Arthur,' Mr Horton said at last, 'what I'm going to tell you is something few people know, and I hope you will follow their example and never discuss it with anyone else.'

'Yes, sir,' said Arthur.

'Ann has told me that you insist on a big ceremony with all the trimmings, and that's what makes the problem. A private ceremony would have left things as they were, and no harm done. Do you follow me?'

'Yes, sir,' said Arthur, lying valiantly. He looked furtively at Ann, but no clue was to be found there. 'Of course, sir,' he said.

'Then, since I'm a man who likes to get to the point quickly I will tell you that I have a son. You're very much like him – in fact, Ann and I were both struck by that resemblance some time ago – but, unfortunately, my son happens to be a thoroughgoing scoundrel. And after one trick too many he was simply bundled off to fend for himself on an allowance I provided. I haven't heard from him since – my lawyer takes care of the details – but if there is to be a big ceremony with everyone on hand to ask questions he must be there. You understand that, of course.'

The room seemed to be closing in around Arthur, and Mr Horton's face was suddenly a diabolic mask floating against the wall.

'Yes, sir,' Arthur whispered.

'That means I must do something now that Ann's been after me to do for years. I have the boy's address; we're all going over right now to meet him, to talk to him, and see if he can't get off to a fresh start with your example before him.'

'Prince Charlie,' said Ann fondly. 'That's what we all used to call him, he was so charming.'

The walls were very close now, the walls of a black chamber,

STH—8

and Ann's face floating alongside her father's. And, strangely enough, there was the face of Mrs Marsh. The kindly garrulous face of Mrs Marsh growing so much bigger than the others.

And a trunk, waiting.

The Betrayers

Between them was a wall. And since it was only a flimsy, jerry-built partition, a sounding board between apartments, Robert came to know the girl that way.

At first she was the sound of footsteps, the small firm rap of high heels moving in a pattern of activity around her room. She must be very young, he thought idly, because at the time he was deep in *Green Mansions*, pursuing the lustrous Rima through a labyrinth of Amazonian jungle. Later he came to know her voice, light and breathless when she spoke, warm and gay when she raised it in chorus to some popular song dinning from her radio. She must be very lovely, he thought then, and after that found himself listening deliberately, and falling more and more in love with her as he listened.

Her name was Amy, and there was a husband, too, a man called Vince who had a flat, unpleasant voice, and a sullen way about him. Occasionally there were quarrels which the man invariably ended by slamming the door of their room and thundering down the stairs as loud as he could. Then she would cry, a smothered whimpering, and Robert, standing close to the wall between them, would feel as if a hand had been thrust inside his chest and was twisting his heart. He would think wildly of the few steps that would take him to her door, the few words that would let her know he was her friend, was willing to do something – anything – to help her. Perhaps, meeting face to face, she would recognize his love. Perhaps –

So the thoughts whirled around and around, but Robert only stood there, taut with helplessness.

And there was no one to confide in, which made it that much harder. The only acquaintances he numbered in the world were the other men in his office, and they would never have understood.

He worked, prosaically enough, in the credit department of one of the city's largest department stores, and too many years there had ground the men around him to a fine edge of cynicism. The business of digging into people's records, of searching for the tax difficulties, the clandestine affairs with expensive women, the touch of larceny in every human being – all that was bound to have an effect, they told Robert, and if he stayed on the job much longer he'd find it out for himself.

What would they tell him now? *A pretty girl next door? Husband's away most of the time? Go on, make yourself at home!*

How could he make them understand that that wasn't what he was looking for? That what he wanted was someone to meet his love halfway, someone to put an end to the cold loneliness that settled in him like a stone during the dark hours each night.

So he said nothing about it to anyone, but stayed close to the wall, drawing from it what he could. And knowing the girl as he had come to, he was not surprised when he finally saw her. The mail for all the apartments was left on a table in the downstairs hallway, and as he walked down the stairs to go to work that morning, he saw her take a letter from the table and start up the stairway toward him.

There was never any question in his mind that this was the girl. She was small and fragile and dark-haired, and all the loveliness he had imagined in her from the other side of the wall was there in her face. She was wearing a loose robe, and as she passed him on the stairway she pulled the robe closer to her breast and slipped by almost as if she were afraid of him. He realized with a start that he had been staring unashamedly, and with his face red he turned down the stairs to the street. But he walked the rest of his way in a haze of wonderment.

He saw her a few times after that, always under the same conditions, but it took weeks before he mustered enough courage to stop at the foot of the stairs and turn to watch her retreating form above: the lovely fine line of ankle, the roundness of calf, the curve of body pressing against the robe. And then as she reached the head of the stairs, as if aware he was watching her, she looked down at him and their eyes met.

For a heart-stopping moment Robert tried to understand what

he read in her face, and then her husband's voice came flat and belligerent from the room. 'Amy,' it said, 'what's holdin' you up!' – and she was gone, and the moment with her.

When he saw the husband he marvelled that she had chosen someone like that. A small, dapper game-cock of a man, he was good-looking in a hard way, but with the skin drawn so tight over his face that the cheekbones jutted sharply and the lips were drawn into a thin menacing line. He glanced at Robert up and down out of the corners of blank eyes as they passed, and in that instant Robert understood part of what he had seen in the girl's face. This man was as dangerous as some half-tamed animal that would snap at any hand laid on him, no matter what its intent. Just being near him you could smell danger, as surely the girl did her every waking hour.

The violence in the man exploded one night with force enough to waken Robert from a deep sleep. It was not the pitch of the voice, Robert realized, sitting up half-dazed in bed, because the words were almost inaudible through the wall; it was the vicious intensity that was so frightening.

He slipped out of bed and laid his ear against the wall. Standing like that, his eyes closed while he strained to follow the choppy phrases, he could picture the couple facing each other as vividly as if the wall had dissolved before him.

'*So you know,*' the man said. '*So what?*'

'*... getting out!*' the girl said.

'*And then tell everybody? Tell the whole world?*'

'*I won't!*' The girl was crying now. '*I swear I won't!*'

'*Think I'd take a chance?*' the man said, and then his voice turned soft and derisive. '*Ten thousand dollars,*' he said. '*Where else could I get it? Digging ditches?*'

'*Better that way! This way ... I'm getting out!*'

His answer was not delivered in words. It came in the form of a blow so hard that when she reeled back and struck the wall, the impact stung Robert's face.

'*Vince!*' she screamed, the sound high and quavering with terror. '*Don't, Vince!*'

Every nerve in Robert was alive now with her pain as the next blow was struck. His fingernails dug into the wall at the hard-breathing noises of scuffling behind it as she was pulled away.

'*Ahh, no!*' she cried out, and then there was the sound of a breath being drawn hoarsely and agonizingly into lungs no longer responsive to it, the thud of a flaccid weight striking the floor, and suddenly silence. A terrible silence.

As if the wall itself were her cold, **de**ad flesh Robert recoiled from it, then stood staring at it in horror. His thoughts twisted and turned on themselves insanely, but out of them loomed one larger and larger so that he had to face it and recognize it.

She had been murdered, and as surely as though he had been standing there beside her he was a witness to it! He had been so close that if the wall were not there he could have reached out his hand and touched her. Done something to help her. Instead, he had waited like a fool until it was too late.

But there was still something to be done, he told himself wildly. And long as this madman in the next room had no idea there was a witness he could still be taken red-handed. A call to the police, and in five minutes...

But before he could take the first nerveless step Robert heard the room next door stealthily come to life again. There was a sound of surreptitious motion, of things being shifted from their place, then, clearly defined, a lifeless weight being pulled along the floor, and the cautious creaking of a door opened wide. It was that last sound which struck Robert with a sick comprehension of what was happening.

The murderer was a monster, but he was no fool. If he could safely dispose of the body now during these silent hours of the night he was, to all intents and purposes, a man who had committed no crime at all!

At his door Robert stopped short. From the hallway came the deliberate thump of feet finding their way down the stairs with the weight dragging behind them. The man had killed once. He was reckless enough in this crisis to risk being seen with his victim. What would such a man do to anyone who confronted him at such a time?

Robert leaned back against his door, his eyes closed tight, a choking constriction in his throat as if the man's hands were already around it. He was a coward, there was no way around it. Faced with the need to show some courage he had discovered he was a rank coward, and he saw the girl's face before him now, not with fear in it, but contempt.

But – and the thought gave him a quick sense of triumph – he could still go to the police. He saw himself doing it, and the sense of triumph faded away. He had heard some noises, and from that he had constructed a murder. The body? There would be none. The murderer? None. Only a man whose wife had left him because he had quarrelled with her. The accuser? A young man who had wild dreams. A perfect fool. In short, Robert himself.

It was only when he heard the click of the door downstairs that he stepped out into the hallway and started down, step by careful step. Halfway down he saw it, a handkerchief, small and crumpled and blotched with an ugly stain. He picked it up gingerly, and holding it up toward the dim light overhead let it fall open. The stain was bright sticky red almost obscuring in one corner the word *Amy* carefully embroidered there. Blood. *Her* blood. Wouldn't that be evidence enough for anyone?

Sure, he could hear the policeman answer him jeeringly, *evidence of a nose-bleed, all right*, and he could feel the despair churn in him.

It was the noise of the car that roused him, and then he flew down the rest of the stairs, but too late. As he pressed his face to the curtain of the front door the car roared away from the kerb, its tail-lights gleaming like malevolent eyes, its licence plate impossible to read in the dark. If he had only been an instant quicker, he raged at himself, only had sense enough to understand that the killer must use a car for his purpose, he could easily have identified it. Now, even that chance was gone. Every chance was gone.

He was in his room pacing the floor feverishly when within a half-hour he heard the furtive sounds of the murderer's return. *And why not*, Robert thought; *he's gotten rid of her, he's safe now, he can go on as if nothing at all had happened.*

If I were only someone who could go into the room and beat the truth out of him, the thought boiled on, *or someone with such wealth or position that I would be listened to . . .*

But all that was as unreal and vaporous as his passion for the girl had been. What weapon of vengeance could he possibly have at his command, a nobody working in a ...

Robert felt the sudden realization wash over him in a cold wave. His eyes narrowed on the wall as if, word by word, the idea were being written on it in a minute hand.

Everyone has a touch of larceny in him – wasn't that what the old hands in his department were always saying? Everyone was suspect. Certainly the man next door, with his bent for violence, his talk of ten thousand dollars come by in some unlikely way, must have black marks on his record that the authorities, blind as they might be, could recognize and act on. If someone skilled in investigation were to strip the man's past down, layer by layer, justice would have to be done. That was the weapon: the dark past itself stored away in the man, waiting only to be ignited!

Slowly and thoughtfully Robert slipped the girl's crumpled handkerchief into an envelope and sealed it. Then, straining to remember the exact words, he wrote down on paper the last violent duologue between murderer and victim. Paper and envelope both went into a drawer of his dresser, and the first step had been taken.

But then, Robert asked himself, what did he know about the man? His name was Vince, and that was all. Hardly information which could serve as the starting point of a search through the dark corridors of someone's past. There must be something more than that, something to serve as a lead.

It took Robert the rest of a sleepless night to hit on the idea of the landlady. A stout and sleepy-eyed woman whose only interest in life seemed to lie in the prompt collection of her rent, she still must have some information about the man. She occupied the rear apartment on the ground floor, and as early in the morning as he dared Robert knocked on her door.

She looked more sleepy-eyed than ever as she pondered his question. 'Them?' she said at last. 'That's the Sniders. Nice people, all right.' She blinked at Robert. 'Not having any trouble with them, are you?'

'No. Not at all. But is that all you can tell me about them? I mean, don't you know where they're from, or anything like that?'

The landlady shrugged. 'I'm sure it's none of my business,' she said loftily. 'All I know is they pay on the first of the month right on the dot, and they're nice respectable people.'

He turned away from her heavily, and as he did so he saw the street door close behind the postman. It was as if a miracle had been passed for him. The landlady was gone, he was all alone with that little heap of mail on the table, and there staring up at him was an envelope neatly addressed to Mrs Vincent Snider.

All the way to his office he kept that envelope hidden away in an inside pocket, and it was only when he was locked in the seclusion of his cubicle that he carefully slit it open and studied its contents. A single page with only a few lines on it, a non-committal message about the family's well-being, and the signature: *Your sister, Celia*. Not much to go on – but wait, there was a return address on the stationery, an address in a small upstate town.

Robert hesitated only a moment, then thrust letter and envelope into his pocket, straightened his jacket, and walked into the office of his superior. Mr Sprague, in charge of the department and consequently the most ulcerated and cynical member of it, regarded him dourly.

'Yes?' he said.

'I'm sorry, sir,' said Robert, 'but I'll need a few days off. You see, there's been a sudden death.'

Mr Sprague sighed at this pebble cast into the smooth pool of his department's routine, but his face fell into the proper sympathetic lines.

'Somebody close?'

'Very close,' said Robert.

The walk from the railroad station to the house was a short one. The house itself had a severe and forbidding air about it, as did the young woman who opened the door in answer to Robert's knock.

'Yes,' she said, 'my sister's name is Amy Snider. Her married name, that is. I'm Celia Thompson.'

'What I'm looking for,' Robert said, 'is some information about her. About your sister.'

The woman looked stricken. 'Something's happened to her?'

'In a way,' Robert said. He cleared his throat hard. 'You see, she's disappeared from her apartment, and I'm looking into it. Now, if you. . .'

'You're from the police?'

'I'm acting for them,' Robert said, and prayed that this ambiguity would serve in place of identification. The prayer was answered, the woman gestured him into the house, and sat down facing him in the bare and uninviting living room.

'I knew,' the woman said, 'I knew something would happen,' and she rocked piteously from side to side in her chair.

Robert reached forward and touched her hand gently. 'How did you know?'

'How? What else could you expect when you drive a child out of her home and slam the door in her face! When you throw her out into the world not even knowing how to take care of herself!'

Robert withdrew his hand abruptly. 'You did *that?*'

'My father did it. *Her* father.'

'But why?'

'If you knew him,' the woman said. 'A man who thinks anything pretty is sinful. A man who's so scared of hellfire and brimstone that he's kept us in it all our lives!

'When she started to get so pretty, and the boys pestering her all the time, he turned against her just like that. And when she had her trouble with that man he threw her out of the house, bag and baggage. And if he knew I was writing letters to her,' the woman said fearfully, 'he'd throw me out, too. I can't even say her name in front of him, the way he is.'

'Look,' Robert said eagerly, 'that man she had trouble with. Was that the one she married? That Vincent Snider?'

'I don't know,' the woman said vaguely. 'I just don't know. Nobody knows except Amy and my father, the way it was kept such a secret. I didn't even know she was married until all of a sudden she wrote me a letter about it from the city.'

'But if your father knows, I can talk to him about it.'

'No! You can't! If he even knew I told you as much as I did. . .'

'But I can't let it go at that,' he pleaded. 'I have to find out about this man, and then maybe we can straighten everything out.'

'All right,' the woman said wearily, 'there is somebody. But not my father, you've got to keep away from him for my sake. There's this teacher over at the high school, this Miss Benson. She's the one to see. And she liked Amy; she's the one Amy mails my letters to, so my father won't know. Maybe she'll tell you, even if she won't tell anybody else. I'll write you a note to her, and you go see her.'

At the door he thanked her, and she regarded him with a hard, straight look. 'You have to be pretty to get yourself in trouble,' she said, 'so its something that'll never bother me. But you find Amy, and you make sure she's all right.'

'Yes,' Robert said. 'I'll try.'

At the school he was told that Miss Benson was the type-writing teacher, that she had classes until three, and that if he wished to speak to her alone he would have to wait until then. So for hours he fretfully walked the few main streets of the town, oblivious of the curious glances of passers-by, and thinking of Amy. These were the streets she had known. These shop windows had mirrored her image. And, he thought with a sharp jealousy, not always alone. There had been boys. Attracted to her, as boys would be, but careless of her, never realizing the prize they had. But if he had known her then, if he could have been one of them...

At three o'clock he waited outside the school building until it had emptied, and then went in eagerly. Miss Benson was a small woman, grey-haired and fluttering, almost lost among the grim ranks of hooded typewriters in the room. After Robert had explained himself and she had read Celia Thompson's note she seemed ready to burst into tears.

'It's wrong of her!' she said. 'It's dreadfully wrong of her to send you to me. She must have known that.'

'But why is it wrong?'

'Why? Because she knows I don't want to talk about it to anyone. She knows what it would cost me if I did, that's why!'

'Look,' Robert said patiently, 'I'm not trying to find out what happened. I'm only trying to find out about this man Amy had trouble with, what his name is, where he comes from, where I can get more information about him.'

'No,' Miss Benson quavered, 'I'm sorry.'

'Sorry,' Robert said angrily. 'A girl disappears, this man may be at the bottom of it, and all you can do is say you're sorry!'

Miss Benson's jaw went slack. 'You mean that he – that he *did* something to her?'

'Yes,' Robert said, 'he did,' and had to quickly catch her arm as she swayed unsteadily, apparently on the verge of fainting.

'I should have known,' she said lifelessly. 'I should have known when it happened that it might come to this. But at the time...'

At the time the girl had been one of her students. A good student – not brilliant, mind you – but a nice girl always trying to do her best. And well brought-up, too, not like so many of the young snips you get nowadays.

That very afternoon when it all happened the girl herself had told Miss Benson she was going to the Principal's office after school hours to get her programme straightened out. Certainly if she meant to do anything wicked she wouldn't have mentioned that, would she? Wasn't that all the evidence anyone needed?

'Evidence?' Robert said in bewilderment.

Yes, evidence. There had been that screaming in the Principal's office, and Miss Benson had been the only one left in the whole school. She had run to the office, flung open the door, and that was how she found them. The girl sobbing hysterically, her dress torn halfway down; Mr Price standing behind her, glaring at the open door, at the incredulous Miss Benson.

'Mr Price?' Robert said. He had the sense of swimming numbly through some gelatinous depths, unable to see anything clearly.

Mr Price, the Principal, of course. He stood glaring at her, his face ashen. Then the girl had fled through the door and Mr Price had taken one step after her, but had stopped short. He had pulled Miss Benson into the office, and closed the door, and then he had talked to her.

The long and the short of what he told her was that the girl was a wanton. She had waltzed into his office, threatened him with blackmail, and when he had put her into her place she had artfully acted out her little scene. But he would be merciful, very merciful. Rather than call in the authorities and blacken the name of the school and of her decent, respectable father he would simply expel her and advise her father to get her out of town promptly.

And, Mr Price had remarked meaningfully, it was a lucky thing indeed that Miss Benson had walked in just in time to be his witness. Although if Miss Benson failed him as a witness it could be highly unlucky for her.

'And he meant it,' Miss Benson said bitterly. 'It's his family runs the town and everything in it. If I said anything of what I really thought, if I dared open my mouth, I'd never get another job anywhere. But I should have talked up, I know I should have, especially after what happened next!'

She had managed to get back to her room at the far end of the corridor although she had no idea of where she got the strength. And as soon as she had entered the room she saw the girl there, lying on the floor beneath the bulletin board from which usually hung the sharp, cutting scissors. But the scissors were in the girl's clenched fist as she lay there, and blood over everything. All that blood over everything.

'She was like that,' Miss Benson said dully. 'If you reprimanded her for even the littlest thing she looked like she wanted to sink through the floor, to die on the spot. And after what she went through it must have been the first thing in her head; just to get rid of herself. It was a mercy of God that she didn't succeed then and there.'

It was Miss Benson who got the doctor, a discreet man, who asked no questions, and it was she who tended the girl after her father had barred his door to her.

'And when she could get around,' Miss Benson said, 'I placed her with this office over at the county seat. She wasn't graduated, of course, or really expert, but I gave her a letter explaining she had been in some trouble and needed a helping hand, and they gave her a job.'

Miss Benson dug her fingers into her forehead. 'If I had only talked up when I should have. I should have known he'd never feel safe, that he'd hound her and hound her until he...'

'But he isn't the one!' Robert said hoarsely. 'He isn't the right man at all!'

She looked at him wonderingly. 'But you said...'

'No,' Robert said helplessly. 'I'm looking for someone else. A different man altogether.'

She shrank back. 'You've been trying to fool me!'

'I swear I haven't.'

'But it doesn't matter,' she whispered. 'If you say a word about this nobody'll believe you. I'll tell them you were lying, you made the whole thing up!'

'You won't have to,' Robert said. 'All you have to do is tell me where you sent her for that job. If you do that you can forget everything else.'

She hesitated, studying his face with bright, frightened eyes. 'All right,' she said at last. 'All right.'

He was about to go when she placed her hand anxiously on his arm. 'Please,' she said. 'You don't think unkindly of me because of all this, do you?'

'No,' Robert said, 'I don't have the right to.'

The bus trip which filled the remainder of the day was a wearing one, the hotel bed that night was no great improvement over the bus seat, and Mr Pardee of *Grace, Grace, & Pardee* seemed to Robert the hardest of all to take. He was a cheery man, too loud and florid to be properly contained by his small office.

He studied Robert's business card with interest. 'Credit research, eh?' he said admiringly. 'Wonderful how you fellas track 'em down wherever they are. Sort of a Northwest Mounted Police just working to keep business healthy, that's what it comes to, doesn't it? And anything I càn do to help...'

Yes, he remembered the girl very well.

'Just about the prettiest little thing we ever had around here,' he said pensively. 'Didn't know much about her job, of course, but you got your money's worth just watching her walk around the office.'

Robert managed to keep his teeth clenched. 'Was there any man she seemed interested in? Someone around the office, maybe, who wouldn't be working here any more? Or even someone outside you could tell me about?'

Mr Pardee studied the ceiling with narrowed eyes. 'No,' he said, 'nobody I can think of. Must have been plenty of men after her, but you'd never get anything out of her about it. Not with the way she was so secretive and all. Matter of fact, her being that way was one of the things that made all the trouble.'

'Trouble?'

'Oh, nothing serious. Somebody was picking the petty cash box every so often, and what with all the rest of the office being so friendly except her it looked like she might be the one. And then that letter she brought saying she had already been in some trouble – well, we just had to let her go.

'Later on,' continued Mr Pardee pleasantly, 'when we found out it wasn't her after all, it was too late. We didn't know where to get in touch with her.' He snapped his fingers loudly. 'Gone, just like that.'

Robert drew a deep breath to steady himself. 'But there must be somebody in the office who knew her,' he pleaded. 'Maybe some girl she talked to.'

'Oh, that,' said Mr Pardee. 'Well, as I said, she wasn't friendly, but now and then she did have her head together with Jenny Rizzo over at the switchboard. If you want to talk to Jenny go right ahead. Anything I can do to help...'

But it was Jenny Rizzo who helped him. A plain girl dressed in defiant bad taste, she studied him with impersonal interest and told him coolly that she had nothing to say about Amy. The kid had taken enough kicking around. It was about time they let her alone.

'I'm not interested in her,' Robert said. 'I'm trying to find out about the man she married. Someone named Vincent Snider. Did you know about him?'

From the stricken look on her face Robert realized exultantly that she did.

'Him!' she said. 'So she went and married him, anyhow!'

'What about it?'

'What about it? I told her a hundred times he was no good. I told her just stay away from him.'

'Why?'

'Because I know his kind. Sharp stuff hanging around with

money in his pocket, you never knew where it came from. The kind of guy's always pulling fast deals, but he's too smart to get caught, that's why!'

'How well did you know him?'

'How well? I knew him from the time he was a kid around my neighbourhood here. Look,' Jenny dug into a desk drawer deep laden with personal possessions. She came out with a handful of snapshots which she thrust at Robert, 'we even used to double-date together, Vince and Amy, and me and my boy friend. Plenty of times I told her right in front of Vince that he was no good, but he gave her such a line she wouldn't even listen. She was like a baby that way; anybody was nice to her she'd go overboard.'

They were not good photographs, but there were Vince and Amy clearly recognizable.

'Could I have one of these?' Robert asked, his voice elaborately casual.

Jenny shrugged. 'Just go ahead and help yourself,' she said, and Robert did.

'Then what happened?' he said. 'I mean, to Vince and Amy?'

'You got me there. After she got fired they both took off. She said something about Vince getting a job downstate a-ways, in Sutton, and that was the last I saw of them. I could just see him working at anything honest, but the way she said it she must have believed him. Anyhow, I never heard from her after that.'

'Could you remember exactly when you saw her last? That time she told you they were going to Sutton?'

Jenny could and did. She might have remembered more, but Robert was out of the door by then, leaving her gaping after him, her mouth wide open in surprise.

The trip to Sutton was barely an hour by bus, but it took another hour before Robert was seated at a large table with the Sutton newspaper files laid out before him. The town's newspaper was a large and respectable one, its files orderly and well-kept. And two days after the date Jenny Rizzo had given him there was the news Robert had hoped to find. Headline news emblazoned all across the top of the first page.

Ten thousand dollars stolen, the news report said. A daring, lone bandit had walked into the Sutton Bank and Trust, had bearded the manager without a soul around knowing it, and had calmly walked out with a small valise containing ten thousand dollars in currency. The police were on the trail. An arrest was expected momentarily...

Robert traced through later dates with his hands shaking. The police had given up in their efforts. No arrest was ever made...

Robert had carefully scissored the photograph so that Vince now stood alone in the picture. The bank manager irritably looked at the picture, and then swallowed hard.

'It's him!' he told Robert incredulously. 'That's the man! I'd know him anywhere. If I can get my hands on him...'

'There's something you'll have to do first,' said Robert.

'I'm not making any deals,' the manager protested. 'I want him, and I want every penny of the money he's got left.'

'I'm not talking about deals,' Robert said. 'All you have to do is put down on paper that you positively identify this man as the one who robbed the bank. If you do that the police'll have him for you tomorrow.'

'That's all?' the man said suspiciously.

'That's all,' Robert said.

He sat again in the familiar room, the papers, the evidence, arranged before him. His one remaining fear had been that in his absence the murderer had somehow taken alarm and fled. He had not breathed easy until the first small, surreptitious noises from next door made clear that things were as he had left them.

Now he carefully studied all the notes he had painstakingly prepared, all the reports of conversations held. It was all here, enough to see justice done, but it was more than that, he told himself bitterly. It was the portrait of a girl who, step by step, had been driven through a pattern of betrayal.

Every man she had dealt with had been an agent of betrayal. Father, school principal, employer, and finally her husband, each was guilty in his turn. Jenny Rizzo's words rang loud in Robert's ears.

Anybody was nice to her she'd go overboard. If he had spoken, if he had moved, he could have been the one. When she turned at the top of the stairs to look at him she might have been waiting for him to speak or move. Now it was too late, and there was no way of letting her know what these papers meant, what he had done for her...

The police were everything Robert had expected until they read the bank manager's statement. Then they read and re-read the statement, they looked at the photograph, and they courteously passed Robert from hand to hand until finally there was a door marked *Lieutenant Kyserling*, and behind it a slender, soft-spoken man.

It was a long story – Robert had not realized until then how long it was or how many details there were to explain – but it was told from start to finish without interruption. At its conclusion Kyserling took the papers, the handkerchief, and the photograph, and pored over them. Then he looked at Robert curiously.

'It's all here,' he said. 'The only thing you left out is why you did it, why you went to all this trouble. What's your stake in this?'

It was not easy to have your most private dream exposed to a complete stranger. Robert choked on the words. 'It's because of her. The way I felt about her.'

'Oh.' Kyserling nodded understandingly. 'Making time with her?'

'No,' Robert said angrily. 'We never even spoke to each other!'

Kyserling tapped his fingers gently on the papers before him.

'Well,' he said, 'it's none of my business anyhow. But you've done a pretty job for us. Very pretty. Matter of fact, yesterday we turned up the body in a car parked a few blocks away from your place. The car was stolen a month ago, there wasn't a stitch of identification on the clothing or anything; all we got is a body with a big wound in it. This business could have stayed up in the air for a hundred years if it wasn't for you walking in with a perfect case made out from A to Z.'

'I'm glad,' Robert said. 'That's the way I wanted it.'

'Yeah,' Kyserling said. 'Any time you want a job on the force you just come and see me.'

Then he was gone from the office for a long while, and when he returned it was in the company of a big, stolid plain-clothes-man who smiled grimly.

'We're going to wrap it up now,' Kyserling told Robert, and gestured at the man.

They went softly up the stairs of the house and stood to the side of the door while Kyserling laid his ear against it for some assurance of sound. Then he briskly nodded to the plain-clothesman and rapped hard.

'Open up!' he called. 'It's the police.'

There was an ear-ringing silence, and Robert's mouth went dry as he saw Kyserling and the plain-clothesman slip the chill blue steel of revolvers from their shoulder holsters.

'I got no use for these cute little games,' growled Kyserling, and suddenly raised his foot and smashed the heel of his shoe hard against the lock of the door. The door burst open. Robert cowed back against the balustrade of the staircase –

And then he saw her.

She stood in the middle of the room facing him wildly, the same look on her face, he knew in that fantastic moment, that she must have worn each time she came face to face with a be-trayer exposed. Then she took one backward step, and suddenly whirled toward the window.

'*Ahh*, no!' she cried, as Robert had heard her cry it out once before, and then she was gone through the window in a sheet of broken glass. Her voice rose in a single despairing shriek, and then was suddenly and mercifully silent.

Robert stood there, the salt of sweat suddenly in his eyes, the salt of blood on his lips. It was an infinity of distance to the window, but he finally got there, and had to thrust Kyserling aside to look down.

She lay crumpled on the sidewalk, and the thick black hair in loose disorder around her face shrouded her from the eyes of the curious.

The plain-clothesman was gone, but Kyserling was still there watching Robert with sympathetic eyes.

'I thought he had killed her,' Robert whispered. 'I could swear he had killed her!'

'It was his body we found,' said Kyserling. 'She was the one who did it.'

'But why didn't you tell me then!' Robert begged. 'Why didn't you let me know!'

Kyserling looked at him wisely. 'Yeah?' he said. 'And then what? You tip her off so that she gets away; then we really got troubles.'

There could be no answer to that. None at all.

'She just cracked up,' Kyserling said reasonably. 'Holed up here like she was, not knowing which way to turn, nobody she could trust... It was in the cards. You had nothing to do with it.'

He went downstairs then, and Robert was alone in her room. He looked around it slowly, at all the things that were left of her, and then very deliberately picked up a chair, held it high over his head, and with all his strength smashed it against the wall...

The House Party

'He's coming around,' said the voice.

He was falling. His hands were outflung against the stone-cold blackness of space, and his body tilted head over heels, heels over head, as he fell. If there were only a way of knowing what was below, of bracing himself against the moment of impact, the terror might not have been so great. This way he was no more than a lump of terror flung into a pit, his mind cowering away from the inevitable while his helpless body descended toward it.

'Good,' the voice said from far away, and it sounded to him as if someone were speaking to him quite calmly and cheerfully from the bottom of the pit. 'Very good.'

He opened his eyes. A glare of light washed in on him suddenly and painfully, and he squinted against it at the figures standing around him, at the faces, partly obscured by a sort of milky haze, looking down at him. He was lying on his back, and from the thrust of the cushions under him he knew he was on the familiar sofa. The milky haze was fading away now, and with it the panic. This was the old house at Nyack, the same living room, the same Utrillo on the wall, the same chandelier glittering over his head. *The same everything*, he thought bitterly, even to the faces around him.

That was Hannah, her eyes bright with tears – she could turn on the tears like a faucet – and her hand was gripping his so hard that his fingers were numb under the pressure. Hannah with the overdeveloped maternal instinct, and only a husband to exercise it on ... That was Abel Roth chewing on a cigar – even at a time like this, that reeking cigar! – and watching him worriedly. Abel with his first successful production in five years, worrying about his investment ... And that was Ben Thayer and Harriet, the eternal bumpkins ... And Jake Hall ... And Tommy McGowan ... All the old familiar faces, the sickening familiar faces.

But there was a stranger, too. A short, stout man with a look of amiable interest on his face, and splendidly bald, with only a tonsure of greying hair to frame his gleaming scalp. He ran his fingers reflectively over his scalp and nodded at Miles.

'How do you feel now?' he asked.

'I don't know,' Miles said. He pulled his hand free of Hannah's and gingerly tried to raise himself to a sitting position. Halfway there he was transfixed by a shocking pain that was driven like a white-hot needle between his ribs. He heard Hannah gasp, and then the stranger's blunt fingers were probing deep into the pain, turning it to liquid, melting it away.

'See?' the man said. 'It's nothing. Nothing at all.'

Miles swung his legs around so that he sat erect on the sofa. He took a deep breath, then another. 'For a second I thought it was my heart,' he said. 'The way it hit me – '

'No, no,' the man said. 'I know what you thought. You can believe me when I say it is of no concern.' And then, as if it explained everything, he said, 'I am Dr Maas. Dr Victor Maas.'

'It was a miracle, darling,' Hannah said breathlessly. 'Dr Maas was the one who found you outside and brought you in. And he's been an absolute angel. If it weren't for him – '

Miles looked at her, and then looked at all the others standing there and watching him with concern. 'Well,' he demanded, 'what *did* happen? What was it? Heart? Stroke? Amnesia? I'm not a child, for God's sake. You don't have to play games with me.'

Abel Roth rolled his cigar from the left-hand corner of his mouth to the right-hand corner. 'You can't blame him for feeling that way, can you, doc? After all, the man is out cold for fifteen minutes, he wants to know where he stands. Maybe there's some kind of check-up you could give him, like blood pressure and stuff like that. Maybe we'd all feel better for it.'

Miles relished that, and relished even more the thought of what he had in store for Abel Roth. 'Maybe we would, Abel,' he said. 'Maybe we've got a theatre sold out sixteen weeks in advance, and the SRO sign up every night. Maybe we've got a real little gold mine to dig so long as I can keep swinging the shovel eight performances a week.'

Abel's face turned red. 'Ah now, Miles,' he said. 'The way you talk – '

'Yes?' Miles said. 'What about the way I talk?'

Ben Thayer shook his head slowly and solemnly. 'If you'd only take the chip off your shoulder for one minute, Miles,' he drawled. 'If you'd try to understand – '

'Please!' Dr Maas said sharply. 'Gentlemen, please!' He frowned at them. 'There is one thing I must make clear. Actually, I am not a medical physician. My interest, so to speak, lies more in the field of psychiatrics, and while I am, perhaps, qualified to make the examination of Mr Owen that you suggest, I have no intention of doing so. For Mr Owen's benefit I will also say that there is no need for me or anyone else to do so. He has my word on that.'

'And Dr Maas, I am sure,' said Miles, 'is an honourable man.' He stood up flexing his knees gingerly, and noting the relief on the faces around him. 'If you want to make yourself at home, doctor, go right ahead. There seems to be some kind of a buffet over there, and while I can't vouch for the food I can promise that the liquor is very, very good.'

The doctor's grin gave him a surprising resemblance to a plump and mischievous boy. 'A delightful suggestion,' he said, and immediately made his way toward the buffet. Abel followed, and, Miles observed, before the doctor had even reached the buffet, the cigar was perilously close to his ear. Abel spent three hours a week on a psychoanalyst's couch, and at least as much time pouring out lists of frightening and inconsequential symptoms to a sleek and well-fed Park Avenue practitioner. Dr Maas, Miles thought with a wry sympathy, was in for some heavy going, whether he knew it or not.

The rest of the circle around the sofa broke up and eddied off, until only Hannah was left. She caught his arm in a panicky grip.

'Are you *sure* you're all right?' she demanded. 'You know you can tell me if there's anything wrong.'

There was something wrong. Every time she caught hold of him like that, tried to draw him close, he had the feeling of a web ensnaring him, closing over him so that he had to fight it savagely.

It had not been like that at the start. She had been so beautiful that he thought in her case it might be different. The rising together, the eating together, the talking together, the endless routine of marriage looked as if it might somehow be bearable as long as it was shared with that loveliness. But then after a year the loveliness had become too familiar, the affection too cloying, the routine too much of a crushing burden.

He had been unconscious for fifteen minutes. He wondered if he had babbled during that time, said something about Lily that could be seized on as a clue. It wasn't of much concern if he had; in fact, it might have been a good way of preparing Hannah for the blow. It was going to be quite a blow, too. He could picture it falling, and it wasn't a pleasant picture.

He shrugged off Hannah's hand. 'There's nothing wrong,' he said, and then could not resist adding, 'unless it's this business of your throwing a house party the one time of the week when I might expect a little peace and quiet.'

'I?' Hannah said uncertainly. 'What did *I* have to do with it?'

'Everything, as long as you've got that damn yen to be the perfect hostess and everybody's friend.'

'They're *your* friends,' she said.

'You ought to know by now that they're not my friends either. I thought I made it clear a hundred different ways that I hate them all, individually and collectively. They're nobody's friends. Why is it my obligation to feed them and entertain them the one time of the week I can get rid of them?'

'I don't understand you,' Hannah said. She looked as if she were about to break into tears. 'I know you bought the house up here so you could get away from everybody, but you were the one – '

The web was closing in again. 'All *right*,' he said. 'All *right*!'

The whole thing didn't matter, anyhow. After he cleared out she could throw a house party every night of the week if she wanted to. She could burn the damn house down if that suited her. It wasn't of any concern to him. He'd had enough of this country-squire life between every Saturday and Monday performance to last him the rest of his life, and, as Lily had once remarked, Central Park had all the trees she wanted to see. Just the realization that he would soon be packed and out of here made any arguments pointless.

He shouldered his way to the buffet past Bob and Liz Gregory who were mooning at each other as if doing it on the radio six mornings a week wasn't enough; past Ben Thayer who was explaining to Jake Hall the trouble he was having with the final act of his new play; past Abel who was saying something to Dr Maas about psychosomatic factors. The doctor had a tall glass in one hand, and a sandwich in the other. 'Interesting,' he was saying. 'Very interesting.'

Miles tried to close his ears to all of them as he poured down two fingers of bourbon. Then he looked at his glass with distaste. The stuff was as flat as warm water, and as unpleasant to the palate. Obviously, one of the local help who took turns cleaning up the house had found the key to the liquor cabinet, and, after nearly emptying the bottle, had done a job on it at the kitchen tap. Damn fool. If you're going to sneak a drink, do it and forget it. But to ruin the rest of the bottle this way ...

Abel poked him in the ribs. 'I was just telling the doctor here,' Abel said, 'if he gets an evening off I'll fix him up with a house seat for *Ambuscade*. I was telling him, if he hasn't seen Miles Owen in *Ambuscade* he hasn't seen the performance of all time. How does that sound to you, Miles?'

Miles was lifting another bottle after making sure its seal was unbroken. He looked at Abel, and then set the bottle down with great care.

'As a matter of fact,' he said, 'I don't know how it sounds to me, Abel. It's something I've wanted to talk to you about, and maybe this is as good a time as any.'

'Talk about what?' said Abel cheerfully, but there was a sudden worry in his eyes, a flickering of premonition on his face.

'It's private business, Abel,' Miles said, and nodded to Dr Maas who stood by interestedly. 'That is, if the doctor will excuse us.'

'Of course, of course,' the doctor said quickly. He waved his glass enthusiastically towards Miles. 'And you were altogether right about the liquor, Mr Owen. It is superb.'

'Fine,' Miles said. 'This way, Abel.'

He pushed his way through the crowd and crossed the room to the library, Abel trailing after him. When he closed the door of the library and switched on a lamp, the chill dampness of the room seemed to soak right into him, and he shivered. Logs and kindling had been laid on the fireplace, and he held a match to it until the wood crackled and caught. Then he lit a cigarette and drew deeply on it. He looked at the cigarette in surprise. There was a flatness about it, a lack of sensation which made him run his tongue over his lips questioningly. He drew again on the cigarette, and then flung it into the fire. First the liquor, he thought, and now this. Dr Maas might be a handy man with Freudian complexes, but the first thing Monday an honest-to-God M.D. would be checking up on this little problem. It is discomforting to find out suddenly that you've lost your capacity to taste anything. Ridiculous maybe, but still discomforting.

Abel was standing at the window. 'Look at that fog, will you. When I brought *Coxcomb* over to London I thought I saw the real thing there, but this makes it look like nothing. You could cut your way through this with a shovel.'

The fog was banked solidly outside the window, stirring in slow waves, sending threads of damp smoke against the glass. Where the threads clung, little beads of water trickled down the pane.

'You get that around here a couple of times a year,' Miles said impatiently. 'And I didn't come in here to talk about the weather.'

Abel turned away from the window and sat down reluctantly in an armchair. 'No, I guess you didn't. All right, Miles, what's bothering you?'

'*Ambuscade*,' Miles said. '*Ambuscade* is what's bothering me.'

Abel nodded wearily. 'It figured. It figured. Well, what particular thing? Your billing? We're using the biggest letters they make. Your publicity? All you have to do is name the time and you have your pick of any TV or radio guest spot in town. Remember what I told you after opening night, Miles? You name it, and if I can get it for you, I will.'

Miles found himself suddenly enjoying the scene. Ordinarily, he had a genuine horror of such scenes. 'Funny,' he said. 'I didn't hear you say anything about money just now, did I? I mean, in all that pretty speech it couldn't have slipped past me, could it?'

Abel sank down in his chair and sighed like a man deeply stricken. 'I thought it would come down to this. Even if I'm paying you twice as much as the biggest star I ever had, I could see it coming, Miles. All right, what's the beef?'

'As a matter of fact,' Miles said, 'there's no beef.'

'No?'

'None at all.'

'What are you getting at?' Abel demanded. 'What's all this about?'

Miles smiled. 'I'm not getting *at* anything, Abel. I'm getting *out*. I'm leaving the show.'

Miles had seen Abel meet more than one crisis before; he could have predicted every action before it took place. The face becoming an impassive mask, the hand searching for a match, the thumbnail flicking the match into a light, the elaborate drawing on the cigar stump, the neat flick of the match across the room. Abel fooled him. The match was snapped with sudden violence between the fingers, and then slowly rolled back and forth, back and forth.

'You're a cute boy, Miles,' Abel said. 'This wouldn't be your idea of a joke, would it?'

'I'm getting out, Abel. Tonight was positively the last appearance. That gives you all day tomorrow to line up another boy for the Monday-night curtain.'

'What other boy?'

'Well, you've got Jay Welker on tap, haven't you? He's been understudying me for five months, and hoping I'd break a leg every night of it.'

'Jay Welker couldn't carry *Ambuscade* one week, and you know it, Miles. Nobody can carry that show but you, and you know that, too.'

Abel leaned forward in his chair and shook his head from side to side unbelievingly. 'And knowing that, you don't give a damn. You'd close the biggest thing on Broadway just like that, and to hell with the whole world, is that it?'

Miles felt his heart starting to pound heavily, his throat tightening. 'Wait a second, Abel, before you start on the dirty words. One thing has already come through pretty well. In all this, you haven't yet asked me why I'm leaving. For all you know I might have some condition that's going to kill me an hour from now, but that would bother you less than keeping your show running! Have you thought about that side of it?'

'What side of it? I was standing right there when the doctor said you were in good shape. What am I supposed to do now? Get affidavits from the American Medical Association?'

'Then it's your idea that I'm pulling out because of a whim?'

'Let's not kid each other, Miles. You did this to Barrow five years ago, you did it to Goldschmidt after that, you did it to Howie Freeman last year, and I know, because that's how I got my chance to grab you for *Ambuscade*. But all the time I figured these others didn't know how to handle you, they didn't see just how much you meant to a show. Now I tell you they were right all along, and I was a prize sucker. They told me you would be going along fine, and then all of a sudden you would get a bug in your ear, and that was it. Bug in your ear, Miles. That's my low, ignorant way of saying whim, which is what it adds up to.'

Abel paused. 'The difference between me and them, Miles, is that I didn't take chances, and that's why you signed the first run-of-the-play contract you ever got since you were a nobody. You think you're walking out on that contract? Think again, my friend.'

Miles nodded. 'All right,' he said thickly, 'I'm thinking. Do you want to know about what?'

'They're your dice, my friend.'

'I'm thinking about eight performances a week, Abel. Eight times a week I say the same lines, walk the same steps, make the same faces. I've done it for five months, which is the biggest break you ever got in your life, but if you had your way I'd be doing it for five years! Right now it's turned into one of those nightmares where you do the same thing over and over without being able to stop, but you wouldn't know about that because *you're* a guy in love with routine! But *I'm* not! After a while it's like being in jail with the key thrown away. What do you tell a man when he can walk out of jail? To stay there and like it?'

'Jail!' Abel cried. 'Tell me somebody in this country who wouldn't give his right eye to be in the kind of jail you're in!'

'Listen,' Miles said. He leaned forward urgently. 'Do you remember before the show opened when we were rehearsing that kitchen scene? Do you remember when we ran through it that night ten times, fifteen times, twenty times? Do you know how I felt then? I felt as if I was plunked right down in hell, and all I would do for eternity was just play that scene over and over again. That's my idea of hell, Abel: a sweet little place where you do the same thing over and over, and they won't even let you go nuts at it, because that would spoil the fun for them. Do you get that? Because if you do, you can see just how I feel about *Ambuscade*!'

'I get it,' Abel said. 'I also get a certain little run-of-the-play contract tucked away in my safe deposit box. If you think rehearsing a scene a few times is hell you'll find out different when Equity lands on you. They look at this a little different from you.'

'Don't try to scare me, Abel.'

'Scare you, hell. I'm going to sue you black and blue, and I'm going to make it stick. I'm dead serious about that, Miles.'

'Maybe. But isn't it hard to sue a man who's too sick to work?'

Abel nodded with grim understanding. 'I figured you'd get around to that angle. I'm the patsy, because to the rest of the world you're sick.' His eyes narrowed. 'And that explains something else, too. That little business of your little blackout on the front doorstep, with a doctor handy, and twenty witnesses to swear to it. I have to hand it to you, Miles, you don't miss a trick. Only it'll take more than a smart trick and a quack doctor to work things your way.'

Miles choked down the rage rising in him. 'If you think that was a trick – !'

'What was a trick?' Harriet Thayer's voice said gaily behind him. Harriet and Ben were standing in the doorway, regarding him with a sort of cheerful curiosity. They made an incongruous couple, Ben's gauntness towering high over Harriet's little-girl fragility, and they had an eager, smalltown friendliness that grated on Miles's nerves like a fingernail drawn down a slate. 'It sounds terribly exciting and interesting,' Harriet said. 'Don't let us stop you.'

Abel pointed at Miles with a shaking forefinger. 'This'll stop you all right,' he said, 'and I'll give it to you in one line. Our friend here is walking out on *Ambuscade*. Maybe *you* can do something to change his mind!'

Ben stared with slow incredulity, and Miles had to marvel, as he had done so many times before, that any man who could write even the few good lines to be found in *Ambuscade* could be so slow on his feet.

'But you can't,' Ben said. 'Your contract runs as long as the play does.'

'Sure,' Abel jeered, 'but he's a sick man. He falls down and has fits. You saw him, didn't you?'

Harriet nodded dumbly. 'Yes, but I never thought – '

'And you were right,' Abel said. 'He's faking it. He's just fed up with making all that money and having all those nice things printed about him, so he's going to close the show. That's all. Just fold it up tight.'

Miles slammed his hand down hard on the arm of Abel's chair. 'All right,' he said, 'now that you've made everything so clear I'll ask you something. Do you think if *Ambuscade* was really a good play that any one person could close it up? Did it ever strike you that no one comes to see your crummy play; they come to see me walk through it? If you gave me *Jabberwocky* to read up there they'd come to see me! Who's to tell a one-man show that he has to keep playing when he doesn't want to!'

'It *is* a good play!' Harriet shouted at him. 'It's the best play you ever acted in, and if you don't know that – '

Miles was shouting himself now. 'Then get someone else to play it! It might be even better that way!'

Ben held his hands out, palms up, in a pleading gesture. 'Now, Miles, you know you've been identified with that part so no one else could take it over,' he said. 'And try to see it my way, Miles. I've been writing fifteen years, and this is the first real break – '

Miles walked up to him slowly. 'You clown,' he said softly. 'Don't you have any self-respect at all?'

When he walked out of the library he quickly slammed the door behind him to forestall any belated answer to that.

The party had broken into several small knots of people scattered around the room, a deafening rise and fall of voices, a haze of blue smoke which lay like a transparent blanket midway between floor and ceiling. Someone, Miles observed, had overturned a drink on the piano; the puddle ran down in a glittering string along the side of the mahogany and was leaving a damp stain on the Wilton rug beneath. Tommy McGowan and his latest, an over-ripe blonde – Norma or Alma or something – sat on the floor shuffling through piles of phonograph records, arranging some into a dangerously high stack and carelessly tossing the others aside. The buffet looked as if a cyclone had hit it; only some empty platters and broken pieces of bread remained amidst the wreckage. From the evidence, Miles thought sardonically, the party would have to be rated a roaring success.

But even the sense of heat and excitement in the room could not erase the chill that he seemed to have brought with him from the library. He rubbed his hands together hard, but this didn't help any, and he felt a small pang of fright at the realization. What if there really were something wrong with him? Lily was not the kind of woman to take gracefully to the role of nursemaid to an invalid. Not that she was wrong about that, as far as he was concerned; if the shoe were on the other foot he couldn't see himself playing any Robert Browning to her Elizabeth Barrett either. Not for Lily or anyone else in the world. In that case it was better not to even bother about a check-up. If there was something, he didn't even want to know about it!

'You are disturbed about something, I think.'

It was Dr Maas. He was leaning casually against the wall, not an arm's length away, his hands thrust into his pockets, his eyes fixed reflectively on Miles. Taking in everything, Miles thought angrily, like some damn scientist looking at a bug under a microscope.

'No,' Miles snapped. Then he thought better of it. 'Yes,' he said. 'As a matter of fact, I am.'

'Ah?'

'I don't feel right. I know you told me I was fine, but I don't feel fine.'

'Physically?'

'Of course, physically! What are you trying to tell me? That it's all in my mind, or some claptrap like that?'

'I am not trying to tell you anything, Mr Owen. You are telling me.'

'All right. Then I want to know what makes you so sure of yourself. No examination, no X-ray, no anything, and you come up with your answer just like that. What's the angle here? Do we somehow get around to the idea that there's nothing wrong physically, but if I put myself in your hands for a nice long expensive psychoanalysis – '

'Stop right there, Mr Owen,' Dr Maas said coldly. 'I will take for granted that your manners are abominable because you are clearly under some pressure. But you should rein in your imagination. I do not practise psychoanalysis, and I never said I did. I am not a healer of any sort. The people I deal with are, unfortunately, always past the point of any cure, and my interest in them, as you can see, must be wholly academic. To be taken for some kind of sharper seeking a victim – '

'Look,' Miles said abruptly, 'I'm sorry. I'm terribly sorry. I don't know what made me go off like that. Maybe it's this party. I hate these damn parties; they always do things to me. Whatever it is, I'm honestly sorry for taking it out on you.'

The doctor nodded gravely. 'Of course,' he said. 'Of course.' Then he nervously ran his fingers over his shining scalp. 'There is something else I should like to say. I am afraid, however, I would risk offending you.'

Miles laughed. 'I think you owe it to me.'

The doctor hesitated, and then gestured toward the library. 'As it happens, Mr Owen, I heard much of what went on in there. I am not an eavesdropper, but the discussion got a little – well, heated, shall we say? – and it was impossible not to overhear it from outside the door here.'

'Yes?' Miles said warily.

'The clue to your condition, Mr Owen, lies in that discussion. To put it bluntly, you are running away. You find what you call routine unbearable, and so you are fleeing from it.'

Miles forced himself to smile. 'What do you mean, what *I* call routine? Is there another word for it in your language?'

'I think there is. I think I would call it responsibility. And since your life, Mr Owen – both your professional and your private life – are very much an open book to the world, I will draw on it and say that most of this life has also been spent fleeing from responsibility of one sort or another. Does it strike you as strange, Mr Owen, that no matter how far and fast you run you always find yourself facing the same problem over and over again?'

Miles clenched and unclenched his fist. 'After all,' he said, 'it's my problem.'

'That is where you're wrong, Mr Owen. When you suddenly leave your role in a play, it affects everyone concerned with that play, and, in turn, everyone concerned with those people. In your relations with women you may move on, but they do not stay motionless either. They move on, too, dangerous to themselves and perhaps to others. Forgive me if I seem sententious, Mr Owen, but you cannot cast pebbles in the water without sending ripples to the far shore.

'That is why when you say *routine*, it is because you are thinking only of yourself caught in a situation. And when I say *responsibility*, I am thinking of everyone else concerned with it.'

'And what's the prescription, Doctor?' Miles demanded. 'To stay sunk in a private little hell because if you try to get away you might step on somebody's toes in the process?'

'Get away?' the doctor said in surprise. 'Do you really think you can get away?'

'You've got a lot to learn, Doctor. Watch me and see.'

'I am watching you, Mr Owen, and I do see. In a wholly academic way, as I said. It is both fascinating and bewildering to see a man trying to flee, as he calls it, his private little hell, while all the time he is carrying it with him.'

Miles's hand was half raised, and then it dropped limp at his side. 'In other words, Doctor,' he said mockingly, 'you're replacing the good old-fashioned sulphur-and-brimstone hell with something even bigger and better.'

The doctor shrugged. 'Of course, you don't believe that.'

'No,' Miles said. 'I don't.'

'I have a confession to make, Mr Owen.' The doctor smiled, and suddenly he was the plump and mischievous boy again. 'I knew you wouldn't. In fact, that is why I felt free to discuss the matter with you.'

'In an academic way, of course.'

'Of course.'

Miles laughed. 'You're quite a man, Doctor. I think I'd like to see more of you.'

'I am sure you will, Mr Owen. But right now I believe that someone is trying to attract your notice. There, by the door.'

Miles followed the doctor's gesturing finger, and his heart stopped. All he could do was pray that no one else had noticed, as he swiftly crossed the room and blocked off the woman who was entering it from the hallway that led to the front door. He thrust her back against the door, and catching hold of her shoulders he shook her once, sharply and angrily.

'Are you crazy?' he demanded. 'Don't you have any more sense than to show up here like this?'

She twisted her shoulders away from his grasp, and carefully brushed at the collar of her coat with her fingertips. The coat had cost Miles a month's pay.

'Aren't you sweet, Miles. Do you invite all your guests in this way?'

Even in the dimness of the hallway she was startling to look at. The sulky lips against the gardenia pallor of the face, the high cheek bones, the slanted eyes darting fire at him. He quailed.

'All right, I'm sorry. I'm sorry. But, my God, Lily, there are two dozen of the biggest mouths on Broadway in that room. If you want the whole world to know about this, why don't you just tip off Winchell?'

She knew when she had him beaten. 'I don't like that, darling. I don't like that at all. I mean, to make it sound as obscene and disgusting as all that. It really isn't supposed to be like that, is it?'

'You know damn well it isn't like that, Lily. But use your head, will you? There is such a thing as discretion.'

'There's also such a thing as working a word to death, darling. And I don't mind telling you that in the last two months you've filled me up to here with that one.'

Miles said angrily, 'I've been trying to make it clear that we'd work this thing out in the right way at the right time. I've already told Abel I am leaving the show. I was going to talk to Hannah, too, but this party has fouled everything up. Tomorrow, when I can be alone with her – '

'Ah, but tomorrow may be a long time away, darling. Much longer than you realize.'

'What exactly does that mean?'

She fumbled through her purse and drew an envelope from it. She waved the envelope back and forth under his nose with a fine air of triumph.

'It means this, Miles. Two pretty little reservations, outward bound, for tomorrow's sailing. You see, you don't have nearly as much time as you thought, do you, darling?'

'Tomorrow! The agent said he couldn't possibly have anything for us within a month!'

'He didn't count on cancellations. This one came through just two hours ago, which is exactly how long it took me to get here. And if it wasn't for that awful fog on the road I would have been here that much sooner. I have the car outside, Miles. You can pack whatever is handy, and get the rest of what you need on the boat. When I go back I expect you to be with me, Miles, because whether you are or not I'll be sailing tomorrow. You can't really blame me for that, can you, darling? After all, none of us are getting any younger.'

He tried to straighten out the aching confusion of his thoughts. He wanted to escape Hannah's web, and now it seemed, somehow or other, there was another waiting to be dropped around him Running, the doctor had said. Always running and never getting anywhere. There was a great weight of weariness in his arms, his legs, his whole body. Running did that to you.

'Well,' Lily said, 'make up your mind, darling.'

He rubbed his hand over his forehead. 'Where's the car?'

'Right across the road.'

'All right,' Miles said, 'you wait in it. Just stay there and don't blow the horn for me, or anything like that. I'll be down in ten minutes. Fifteen minutes at the most. Most of my stuff is in town, anyhow. We'll pick it up on the way to the boat.'

He opened the door and gently pushed her toward it.

'You'll have to feel your way to the car, Miles. I've never seen anything like what's outside.'

'I'll find it,' he said. 'You just wait there.'

He closed the door, then leaned against it fighting the sickness that kept rising to his throat. The loud voices in the next room, the shrieks of idiot laughter that now and then cut through it, the roar of music from the phonograph tuned at its greatest volume – everything seemed conspiring against him, not allowing him to be alone, not allowing him to think things out.

He went up the stairs almost drunkenly, and into the bedroom. He pulled out his valise, and then at random started cramming it full. Shirts, socks, the contents of the jewel case on his dresser. He thrust down hard with all his weight, making room for more.

'What are you doing, Miles?'

He didn't look up. He knew exactly what the expression on her face would be, and he didn't want to meet it then. It would have been too much.

'I'm leaving, Hannah.'

'With that woman?' Her voice was a vague, uncomprehending whisper.

He had to look at her then. Her eyes stared at him, enormous against the whiteness of her skin. Her hand fumbled with the ornament at her breast. It was the silver mask of comedy he had picked up for her on Fifth Avenue a week before their marriage.

She said wonderingly, 'I saw you with her in the hallway. I wasn't prying or anything like that, Miles, but when I asked the doctor where you were – '

'Stop it!' Miles shouted. 'What do you have to apologize for!'

'But she's the one, isn't she?'

'Yes, she's the one.'

'And you want to go away with her?'

His hands were on the lid of the valise. He rested his weight on them, head down, eyes closed.

'Yes,' he said at last. 'That's what it comes to.'

'No!' she cried with a sudden fervour. 'You don't really want to. You know she's not good for you. You know there's nobody in the whole world as good for you as I am!'

He pressed the lid of the valise down. The lock caught with a tiny click.

'Hannah, it would have been better for you not to have come up just now. I would have written to you, explained it somehow – '

'Explained it? When it would be too late? When you'd know

what a mistake you made? Miles, listen to me. Listen to me, Miles. I'm talking to you out of all my love. It would be a terrible mistake.'

'I'll have to be the judge of that, Hannah.'

He stood up, and she came toward him, her fingers digging into his arms frantically. 'Look at me, Miles,' she whispered. 'Can't you see how I feel? Can't you understand that I'd rather have the both of us dead than to have you go away like this and leave the whole world empty for me!'

It was horrible. It was the web constricting around him so hard that it was taking all his strength to pull himself free. But he did, with a brutal effort, and saw her fall back against the dresser. Then she suddenly wheeled toward it, and when she faced him again he saw the pistol levelled at him. It shone a cold, deadly blue in her hand, and then he realized that her hand was trembling so violently that the gun must be frightening her as much as it did him. The whole grotesquerie of the scene struck him full force, melting away the fear, filling him with a sense of outrage.

'Put that thing down,' he said.

'No.' He could hardly hear her. 'Not unless you tell me that you're not going.'

He took a step toward her, and she shrank farther back against the dresser, but the gun remained levelled at him. She was like a child afraid someone was going to trick her out of a toy. He stopped short, and then shrugged with exaggerated indifference.

'You're making a fool of yourself, Hannah. People are paid for acting like this on the stage. They're not supposed to make private shows of themselves.'

Her head moved from side to side in a slow, aimless motion. 'You still don't believe me, do you, Miles?'

'No,' he said. 'I don't.'

He turned his back on her, half expecting to hear the sudden explosion, feel the impact between his shoulder blades, but there was nothing. He picked up the valise and walked to the door.

'Good-bye. Hannah,' he said. He didn't turn his head to look at her.

The weakness in his knees made each step a trial. He stopped at the foot of the staircase to shift the valise from one hand to the other, and saw Dr Maas standing there, hat in hand, a topcoat thrown over his arm.

'Ah?' said the doctor inquiringly. 'So you, too, are leaving the party, Mr Owen?'

'Party?' Miles said, and then laughed short and sharp. 'Leaving the nightmare, if you don't mind, Doctor. I hate to tell this to a guest, but I think you'll understand me when I say that this past hour has been a nightmare that gets thicker and thicker. That's what I'm leaving, Doctor, and you can't blame me for being happy about it.'

'No, no,' said the Doctor. 'I quite understand.'

'The car is waiting for me outside. If I can give you a lift anywhere – ?'

'Not at all,' the doctor said. 'I really do not have far to go.'

They went to the doorway together and stepped outside. The fog moved in on them, cold and wet, and Miles turned up his jacket collar against it.

'Rotten weather,' he said.

'Terrible,' the doctor agreed. He glanced at his watch, and then lumbered down the steps to walk like a walrus disappearing into a snowbank. 'I'll be seeing you, Mr Owen,' he called.

Miles watched him go, then lifted the valise and went down the steps himself, burying his nose in his collar against the smothering dampness all around him. He was at the bottom step when he heard the sibilance of the door opening behind him, the faraway whisper of danger in his bones.

He turned, and, as he knew it would be, there was Hannah standing at the open door, still holding the gun. But the gun was gripped tightly in both hands now, and the menace of it was real and overwhelming.

'I tried to make you understand, Miles,' she said, like a child saying the words. 'I tried to make you understand.'

He flung his arms out despairingly.

'No!' he cried wildly. 'No!'

And then there was the roar of the explosion in his ears, the gout of flame leaping out toward him, the crushing impact against his chest, and the whole world dissolving. In it, only one thing stood sharp and definable: the figure of the doctor bending over him, the face strangely Satanic in its cruel indifference.

For that single moment Miles understood everything. He had been here before. He had lived this hour a thousand times before, and would live it again and again for all eternity. The curtain was falling now, but when it rose again the stage would be set once more for the house party. Because he was in Hell, and the most terrible thing of all, the terror which submerged all others, was this moment of understanding given him so that he could know this, and could see himself crawling the infinite treadmill of his doom. Then the darkness closed in with a rush, blotting out all understanding – until next time ...

'*He's coming around,*' *said the voice.*
He was falling. His hands were outflung ...

Broker's Special

It was the first time in a good many years that Cornelius, a Wall Street broker, had made the homeward trip in any train other than the Broker's Special. The Special was his kind of train; the passengers on it were his kind of people. Executives, professionals, men of substance and dignity who could recognize each other without introductions, and understand each other without words.

If it weren't for the Senator's dinner party, Cornelius reflected. But the Senator had insisted, so there was no escape from that abomination of abominations, the midweek dinner party. And, of course, no escape from the necessity of taking an earlier train home to the tedium of dressing, and an evening of too much food, too much liquor, and all the resultant misery the next morning.

Filled with this depressing thought Cornelius stepped down heavily from the train to the familiar platform and walked over to his car. Since Claire preferred the station wagon, he used the sedan to get to and from the station. When they were first married two years ago she had wanted to chauffeur him back and forth, but the idea had somehow repelled him. He had always felt there was something vaguely obscene about the way other men publicly kissed their wives good-bye in front of the station every morning, and the thought of being placed in their position filled him with a chilling embarrassment. He had not told this to Claire, however. He had simply told her he had not married her to obtain a housekeeper or chauffeur. She was to enjoy her life, not fill it with unnecessary duties.

Ordinarily, it was no more than a fifteen-minute drive through the countryside to the house. But now, in keeping with the already exasperating tenor of the day's events, he met an unexpected delay. A mile or so past where the road branched off from the highway it crossed the main line of the railroad. There was no guard or crossing gate here, but a red light, and a bell which was ringing an insistent warning as Cornelius drove up. He braked the car, and sat tapping his fingers restlessly on the steering wheel while the endless, clanking length of a freight went by. And then, before he could start the car again, he saw them.

It was Claire and a man. His wife and some man in the station wagon roaring past him into town. And the man was driving – seated big and blond and arrogant behind the wheel like a Viking – with one arm around Claire who, with eyes closed, rested her head on his shoulder. There was a look on her face, too, such as Cornelius had never seen there before, but which he had sometimes dreamed of seeing. They passed by in a flash, but the picture they made was burned as brilliant in his mind as a photograph on film.

He would not believe it, he told himself incredulously; he refused to believe it! But the picture was there before him, growing clearer each second, becoming more and more terribly alive as he watched it. The man's arm possessing her. Her look of acceptance. Of sensual acceptance.

He was shaking uncontrollably now, the blood pounding in his head, as he prepared to turn the car and follow them. Then he felt himself go limp. Follow them where? Back to town undoubtedly, where the man would be waiting for the next train to the city. And then what? A denunciation in the grand style? A scene? A public humiliation for himself as much as for them?

He could stand anything, but not such humiliation. It had been bad enough when he had first married Claire and realized his friends were laughing at him for it. A man in his position to marry his secretary, and a girl half his age at that! Now he knew what they had been laughing at, but he had been blind then. There had been such an air of cool formality about her when she carried on her duties in the office; she sat with such prim dignity when she took his notes; she had dressed so modestly – and when he had first invited her to dinner she had reddened with the flustered naivete of a young girl being invited on her first date. Naivete! And all the time, he thought furiously, she must have been laughing at me. She, along with the rest of them.

He drove to the house slowly, almost blindly. The house was

empty, and he realized that, of course, it was Thursday, the servant's day off, which made it the perfect day for Claire's purpose. He went directly to the library, sat down at the desk there, and unlocked the top drawer. His gun was in that drawer, a shortbarrelled .38, and he picked it up slowly, hefting its cold weight in his hand, savouring the sense of power it gave him. Then abruptly his mind went back to something Judge Hilliker had once told him, something strangely interesting that the old man had said while sharing a seat with him on the Broker's Special.

'Guns?' Hilliker had said. 'Knives? Blunt instruments? You can throw them all out of the window. As far as I'm concerned there is just one perfect weapon – an automobile. Any automobile in good working order. Why? Because when an automobile is going fast enough it will kill anyone it hits. And if the driver gets out and looks sorry he'll find that he's the one getting everybody's sympathy, and not that bothersome corpse on the ground who shouldn't have been in the way anyhow. As long as the driver isn't drunk or flagrantly reckless he can kill anybody in this country he wants to, and suffer no more than a momentary embarrassment and a penalty that isn't even worth worrying about.

'Think it over, man,' the Judge continued: 'to most people the automobile is some sort of god, and if God happens to strike you down it's your hard luck. As for me, when I cross a street I just say a little prayer.'

There was more of that in Judge Hilliker's mordant and longwinded style, but Cornelius had no need to remember it. What he needed he now had, and very carefully he put the gun back in the drawer, slid the drawer shut, and locked it.

Claire came in while he still sat brooding at the desk, and he forced himself to regard her with cold objectivity – this radiantly lovely woman who was playing him for a fool, and who now stood wide-eyed in the doorway with an incongruously large bag of groceries clutched to her.

'I saw the car in the garage,' she said breathlessly. 'I was afraid something was wrong. That you weren't feeling well. ...'

'I feel very well.'

'But you're home so early. You've never come this early before.'

'I've always managed to refuse invitations to midweek dinner parties before.'

'Oh, Lord!' she gasped. 'The dinner! It never even entered my mind. I've been so busy all day. ...'

'Yes?' he said. 'Doing what?'

'Well, everyone's off today, so I took care of the house from top to bottom, and then when I looked in the pantry and saw we needed some things I ran into town for them.' She gestured at the bulky paper bag with her chin. 'I'll have your bath ready, and your things laid out as soon as I put this stuff away.'

Watching her leave he felt an honest admiration for her. Another woman would have invented a visit to a friend who might, at some later time, accidentally let the cat out of the bag. Or another woman would not have thought to burden herself with a useless package to justify a trip into town. But not Claire, who was evidently as clever as she was beautiful.

And she *was* damnably attractive. His male friends may have laughed behind his back, but in their homes she was always eagerly surrounded by them. When he entered a roomful of strangers with her he saw how all men's eyes followed her with a frankly covetous interest. No, nothing must happen to her; nothing at all. It was the man who had to be destroyed, just as one would destroy any poacher on his preserves, any lunatic who with axe in hand ran amok through his home. Claire would have to be hurt a little, would have to be taught her lesson, but that would be done most effectively through what happened to the man.

Cornelius learned very quickly that his plans would have to take in a good deal more than the simple act of waylaying the man and running him down. There were details, innumerable details covering every step of the way before and after the event, which had to be jigsawed into place bit by bit in order to make it perfect.

In that respect, Cornelius thought gratefully, the Judge had been far more helpful than he had realized in his irony. Murder by automobile was the perfect murder, because, with certain details taken care of, it was not even murder at all! There was the victim, and there was the murderer standing over him, and the whole thing would be treated with perfunctory indifference. After all, what was one more victim among the thirty thousand each year? He was a statistic, to be regarded with some tongue-clicking and a shrug of helplessness.

Not by Claire, of course. Coincidence can be stretched far, but hardly far enough to cover the case of a husband's running down his wife's lover. And that was the best part of it. Claire would know, but would be helpless to say anything, since saying anything must expose her own wrongdoing. She would spend her life day after day, knowing that she had been found out, knowing that a just vengeance had been exacted, and standing forewarned against any other such temptations that might come her way.

But what of the remote possibility that she might choose to speak out and expose herself? There, Cornelius reflected, fitting another little piece of the jigsaw into place, coincidence would instantly go to work for him. If there was no single shred of evidence that he had ever suspected her affair, or that he had ever seen the man before, the accident *must* be regarded by the law as coincidence. Either way his position was unassailable.

It was with this in mind that he patiently and singlemindedly went to work on his plans. He was tempted at the start to call in some professional investigator who could promptly and efficiently bring him the information he wanted, but after careful consideration he put this idea aside. A smart investigator might easily put two and two together after the accident. If he were honest he might go to the authorities with his suspicions; if he were dishonest he might be tempted to try blackmail. Obviously, there was no way of calling in an outsider without risking one danger or the other. And nothing, nothing at all, was going to be risked here.

So it took Cornelius several precious weeks to glean the information he wanted, and, as he admitted to himself, it might have taken even longer had not Claire and the man maintained such an unfailing routine. Thursday was the one day of the week on which the man would pay his visits. Then, a little before the city-bound train arrived at the station, Claire would drive the station wagon into an almost deserted sidestreet a block from the Plaza.

In the car the couple would kiss with an intensity that made Cornelius's flesh crawl.

As soon as the man left the car Claire would drive swiftly away, and the man would walk briskly to the Plaza, make his way through the cars parked at the kerb there, cross the Plaza obviously sunk in his own thoughts and with only half an eye for passing traffic, and would enter the station. The third time Cornelius witnessed this performance he could have predicted the man's every step with deadly accuracy.

Occasionally, during this period, Claire mentioned that she was going to the city to do some shopping, and Cornelius took advantage of this as well. He was standing in a shadow of the terminal's waiting room when her train pulled in, he followed her at a safe distance to the street, his cab trailed hers almost to the door of the shabby apartment house where the man lived. The man was sitting on the grimy steps of the house, obviously waiting for her. When he led her into the house, as Cornelius bitterly observed, they held hands like a pair of school children, and then was a long wait, a wait which took up most of the afternoon; but Cornelius gave up waiting before Claire reappeared.

The eruption of fury he knew after that scene gave him the idea of staging the accident there on the city streets the next day, but Cornelius quickly dismissed the thought. It would mean driving the car into the city, which was something he never did, and that would be a dangerous deviation from his own routine. Besides, city tabloids, unlike his staid local newspaper, sometimes publicized automobile accidents not only by printing the news of them, but also by displaying pictures of victim and culprit on their pages. He wanted none of that. This was a private affair. Strictly private.

No, there was no question that the only place to settle matters was right in the Plaza itself, and the more Cornelius reviewed his plans in preparation for the act the more he marvelled at how flawless they were.

Nothing could conceivably go wrong. If by some mischance he struck down the man without killing him, his victim would be in the same position as Claire: unable to speak openly without exposing himself. If he missed the man entirely he was hardly in the dangerous position of an assassin who misses his victim and is caught with the gun or knife in his hand. An automobile wasn't a weapon; the affair would simply be another close call for a careless pedestrian.

However, he wanted no close calls, and to that end he took to parking the car somewhat farther from the station than he ordinarily did. The extra distance, he estimated, would allow him to swing the car across the Plaza in an arc which would meet the man as he emerged from between the parked cars across the street. That would just about make explanations uncalled-for. A man stepping out from between parked cars would be more in violation of the law than the driver who struck him!

Not only did he make sure to set the car at a proper distance from the station entrance, but Cornelius also took to backing it into place as some other drivers did. Now the front wheels were facing the Plaza, and he could quickly get up all the speed he wanted. More than that, he would be facing the man from the instant he came into sight.

The day before the one he had chosen for the final act, Cornelius waited until he was clear of traffic on his homeward drive, and then stopped the car on a deserted part of the road, letting the motor idle. Then he carefully gauged the distance to a tree some thirty yards ahead; this, he estimated, would be the distance across the Plaza. He started the car and then drove it as fast as he could past the tree, the big machine snarling as it picked up speed. Once past the tree he braced himself, stepped hard on the brake, and felt the pressure of the steering wheel against his chest as the car slewed to a shrieking stop.

That was it. That was all there was to it...

He left the office the next day at the exact minute he had set for himself. After his secretary had helped him on with his coat he turned to her as he had prepared himself to do and made a wry face.

'Just not feeling right,' he said. 'Don't know what's wrong with me, Miss Wynant.'

And, as he knew good secretaries were trained to do, she frowned worriedly at him and said, 'If you didn't work so hard, Mr Bolinger...'

He waved that aside brusquely. 'Nothing that getting home early to a good rest won't cure. Oh,' he slapped at the pockets of his coat, 'my pills, Miss Wynant. They're in the top drawer over there.'

They were only a few aspirins in an envelope, but it was the impression that counted. A man who was not feeling well had that much more justification for a mishap while he was driving.

The early train was familiar to him now; he had ridden on it several times during the past few weeks, but always circumspectly hidden behind a newspaper. Now it was to be different. When the conductor came through to check his commutation ticket, Cornelius was sitting limp in his seat, clearly a man in distress.

'Conductor,' he asked, 'if you don't mind, could you get me some water?'

The conductor glanced at him and hastily departed. When he returned with a dripping cup of water Cornelius slowly and carefully removed an aspirin from the envelope and washed it down gratefully.

'If there's anything else,' the conductor said, 'just you let me know.'

'No,' Cornelius said, 'no, I'm a little under the weather, that's all.'

But at the station the conductor was there to lend him a solicitous hand down, and dally briefly. 'You're not a regular, are you?' the conductor said. 'At least, not on this train?'

Cornelius felt a lift of gratification. 'No,' he said, 'I've only taken this train once before. I usually travel on the Broker's Special.'

'Oh.' The conductor looked him up and down, and grinned. 'Well, that figures,' he said. 'Hope you found our service as good as the Special's.'

In the small station Cornelius sat down on a bench, his head resting against the back of the bench, his eyes on the clock over the ticket agent's window. Once or twice he saw the agent glance worriedly through the window at him, and that was fine. What was not so fine was the rising feeling in him, a lurching nervousness in his stomach, a too-heavy thudding of his heart in his chest. He had allowed himself ten minutes here; each minute found the feeling getting more and more oppressive. It was an effort to contain himself, to prevent himself from getting to his feet and rushing out to the car before the minute hand of the clock had touched the small black spot that was his signal.

Then, on the second, he got up, surprised at the effort it required to do this, and slowly walked out of the station, the agent's eyes following him all the way, and down past the station to the car. He climbed behind the wheel, closed the door firmly after him, and started the motor. The soft purring of the motor under his feet sent a new strength up through him. He sat there soaking it up, his eyes fixed on the distance across the Plaza.

When the man first appeared, moving with rapid strides toward him, it struck Cornelius in some strange way that the tall, blond figure was like a puppet being drawn by an invisible wire to his destined place on the stage. Then, as he came closer, it was plain to see that he was smiling broadly, singing aloud in his exuberance of youth and strength – and triumph. That was the key which unlocked all paralysis, which sent the motor roaring into furious life.

For all the times he had lived the scene in his mind's eye, Cornelius was unprepared for the speed with which it happened. There was the man stepping out from between the cars, still blind to everything. There was Cornelius's hand on the horn, the ultimate inspiration, a warning that could not possibly be heeded, and more than anything else an insurance of success. The man swung toward the noise, his face all horror, his hands out-thrust as if to fend off what was happening. There was the high-pitched scream abruptly cut off by the shock of impact, more violent than Cornelius had ever dreamed, and then everything dissolving into the screech of brakes.

The Plaza had been deserted before it had happened; now, people were running from all directions, and Cornelius had to push his way through them to catch a glimpse of the body.

'Better not look,' someone warned, but he did look, and saw the crumpled form, the legs scissored into an unnatural position, the face greying as he watched. He swayed, and a dozen helping hands reached out to support him, but it was not weakness which affected him now, but an overwhelming, giddy sense of victory, a sense of victory heightened by the voices around him.

'Walked right into it with his eyes wide open.'

'I could hear that horn a block away.'

'Drunk, maybe. The way he stood right there. ...'

The only danger now lay in overplaying his hand. He had to watch out for that, had to keep fitting piece after piece of the plan together, and then there would be no danger. He sat in the car while a policeman questioned him with official gravity, and he knew from the growing sympathy in the policeman's voice that he was making the right impression.

No, he was free to go home if he wished. Charges, of course, had to be automatically preferred against him, but the way things looked. ... Yes, they would be glad to phone Mrs Bolinger. They could drive him home, but if he preferred to have her do it. ...

He had allowed time enough for her to be at home when the call was made, and he spent the next fifteen minutes with the crowd staring at him through the car window with a morbid and sympathetic curiosity. When the station wagon drew up nearby, a lane magically appeared through the crowd; when Claire was at his side the lane disappeared.

Even frightened and bewildered, she was a beautiful woman, Cornelius thought, and, he had to admit to himself, she knew how to put on a sterling show of wifely concern and devotion, false as it was. But perhaps that was because she didn't know yet, and it was time for her to know.

He waited until she had helped him into the station wagon, and when she sat down in the driver's seat he put an arm tight around her.

'Oh, by the way, officer,' he asked with grave anxiety through the open window. 'Did you find out who the man was? Did he have any identification on him?'

The policeman nodded. 'Young fellow from the city,' he said, 'so we'll have to check up on him down there. Name of Lundgren. Robert Lundgren, if his card means anything.'

Against his arm Cornelius felt, rather than heard, the choked gasp, felt the uncontrollable small shivering. Her face was as grey as that of the man's out there in the street. 'All right, Claire,' he said softly. 'Let's go home.'

She drove by instinct out through the streets of the town. Her face was vacuous, her eyes set and staring. He was almost grateful when they reached the highway, and she finally spoke in a quiet and wondering voice. 'You knew,' she said. 'You knew about it, and you killed him for it.'

'Yes,' Cornelius said, 'I knew about it.'

'Then you're crazy,' she said dispassionately, her eyes still fixed ahead of her. 'You must be crazy to kill someone like that.'

Her even, informative tone fired his anger as much as what she was saying.

'It was justice,' he said between his teeth. 'It was coming to him.'

She was still remote. 'You don't understand.'

'Don't understand what?'

She turned toward him, and he saw that her eyes were glistening wet. 'I knew him before I ever knew you, before I ever started working in the office. We always went together; it didn't seem as if there was any point living if we couldn't be together.' She paused only a fraction of a second. 'But things didn't go right. He had big ideas that didn't make any money, and I couldn't stand that. I was born poor, and I couldn't stand marrying poor and dying poor. . . . That's why I married you. And I tried to be a good wife – you'll never know how hard I tried! – but that wasn't what you wanted. You wanted a showpiece, not a wife; something to parade around in front of people so that they could admire you for owning it, just like they admire you for everything else you own.'

'You're talking like a fool,' he said harshly. 'And watch the road. We turn off here.'

'Listen to me!' she said. 'I was going to tell you all about it. I was going to ask for a divorce. Not a penny to go with it, or anything like that – just the divorce so that I could marry him and make up for all the time I had thrown away! That's what I told him today, and if you had only asked – only talked to me – '

She would get over it, he thought. It had been even more serious than he had realized, but, as the saying went, *all passes*. She had nothing to trade her marriage for any longer; when she understood that clearly they would make a new start. It was a miracle that he had thought of using the weapon he had, and that he had used it so effectively. *A perfect weapon*, the Judge had said. He'd never know how perfect.

It was the warning clangour of the bell at the grade crossing that jarred Cornelius from his reverie – that, and the alarming realization that the car's speed was not slackening at all. Then everything else was submerged by the angry bawling of a Diesel horn, and when he looked up incredulously, it was to the raging mountain of steel that was the Broker's Special hurling itself over the crossing directly ahead.

'Watch out!' he cried out wildly. 'My God, what are you doing!'

In that last split second, when her foot went down hard on the accelerator, he knew.

The Moment of Decision

Hugh Lozier was the exception to the rule that people who are completely sure of themselves cannot be likeable. We have all met the sure ones, of course – those controlled but penetrating voices which cut through all others in a discussion, those hard fore-fingers jabbing home opinions on your chest, those living Final Words on all issues – and I imagine we all share the same amalgam of dislike and envy for them. Dislike, because no one likes to be shouted down or prodded in the chest, and envy, because everyone wishes he himself were so rich in self-assurance that he could do the shouting down and prodding.

For myself, since my work took me regularly to certain places in this atomic world where the only state was confusion and the only steady employment that of splitting political hairs, I found absolute judgements harder and harder to come by. Hugh once observed of this that it was a good thing my superiors in the Department were not cut of the same cloth, because God knows what would happen to the country then. I didn't relish that, but – and there was my curse again – I had to grant him his right to say it.

Despite this, and despite the fact that Hugh was my brother-in-law – a curious relationship when you come to think of it – I liked him immensely, just as everyone else did who knew him. He was a big, good-looking man, with clear blue eyes in a ruddy face, and with a quick, outgoing nature eager to appreciate whatever you had to offer. He was overwhelmingly generous, and his generosity was of that rare and excellent kind which makes you feel as if you are doing the donor a favour by accepting it.

I wouldn't say he had any great sense of humour, but plain good humour can sometimes be an adequate substitute for that, and in Hugh's case it was. His stormy side was largely reserved for those times when he thought you might have needed his help in something and failed to call on him for it. Which meant that ten minutes after Hugh had met you and liked you, you were expected to ask him for anything he might be able to offer. A month or so after he married my sister Elizabeth she mentioned to him my avid interest in a fine Copley he had hanging in his gallery at Hilltop, and I can still vividly recall my horror when it suddenly arrived, heavily crated and with his gift card attached, at my barren room-and-a-half. It took considerable effort, but I finally managed to return it to him by forgoing the argument that the picture was undoubtedly worth more than the entire building in which I lived and by complaining that it simply didn't show to advantage on my wall. I think he suspected I was lying, but being Hugh he would never dream of charging me with that in so many words.

Of course, Hilltop and the two hundred years of Lozier tradition that went into it did much to shape Hugh this way. The first Loziers had carved the estate from the heights overlooking the river, had worked hard and flourished exceedingly; its successive generations had invested their income so wisely that money and position eventually erected a towering wall between Hilltop and the world outside. Truth to tell, Hugh was very much a man of the eighteenth century who somehow found himself in the twentieth, and simply made the best of it.

Hilltop itself was almost a replica of the celebrated, but long untenanted, Dane house near by, and was striking enough to open anybody's eyes at a glance. The house was weathered stone, graceful despite its bulk, and the vast lawns reaching to the river's edge were tended with such fanatic devotion over the years that they had become carpets of purest green which magically changed lustre under any breeze. Gardens ranged from the other side of the house down to the groves which half hid the stables and out-buildings, and past the far side of the groves ran the narrow road which led to town. The road was a courtesy road, each estate holder along it maintaining his share, and I think it safe to say that for all the crushed rock he laid in it Hugh made less use of it by far than any of his neighbours.

Hugh's life was bound up in Hilltop; he could be made to leave it only by dire necessity; and if you did meet him away from it you were made acutely aware that he was counting off the minutes until he could return. And if you weren't wary you would more than likely find yourself going along with him when he did return, and totally unable to tear yourself away from the place while the precious weeks rolled by. I know. I believe I spent more time at Hilltop than at my own apartment after my sister brought Hugh into the family.

At one time I wondered how Elizabeth took to this marriage, considering that before she met Hugh she had been as restless and flighty as she was pretty. When I put the question to her directly, she said, 'It's wonderful, darling. Just as wonderful as I knew it would be when I first met him.'

It turned out that their first meeting had taken place at an art exhibition, a showing of some ultra-modern stuff, and she had been intently studying one of the more bewildering concoctions on display when she became aware of this tall, good-looking man staring at her. And, as she put it, she had been about to set him properly in his place when he said abruptly, 'Are you admiring that?'

This was so unlike what she had expected that she was taken completely aback. 'I don't know,' she said weakly. 'Am I supposed to?'

'No,' said the stranger, 'it's damned nonsense. Come along now, and I'll show you something which isn't a waste of time.'

'And,' Elizabeth said to me, 'I came along like a pup at his heels, while he marched up and down and told me what was good and what was bad, and in a good loud voice, too, so that we collected quite a crowd along the way. Can you picture it, darling?'

'Yes,' I said, 'I can.' By now I had shared similar occasions with Hugh, and learned at firsthand that nothing could dent his cast-iron assurance.

'Well,' Elizabeth went on, 'I must admit that at first I was a little put off, but then I began to see that he knew exactly what he was talking about, and that he was terribly sincere. Not a bit self-conscious about anything, but just eager for me to understand things the way he did. It's the same way with everything. Everybody else in the world is always fumbling and bumbling over deciding anything – what to order for dinner, or how to manage his job, or whom to vote for – but Hugh always *knows*. It's *not* knowing that makes for all those nerves and complexes and things you hear about, isn't that so? Well, I'll take Hugh, thank you, and leave everyone else to the psychiatrists.'

So there it was. An Eden with flawless lawns and no awful nerves and complexes, and not even the glimmer of a serpent in the offing. That is, not a glimmer until the day Raymond made his entrance on the scene.

We were out on the terrace that day, Hugh and Elizabeth and I, slowly being melted into a sort of liquid torpor by the August sunshine, and all of us too far gone to make even a pretence at talk. I lay there with a linen cap over my face, listening to the summer noises around me and being perfectly happy.

There was the low, steady hiss of the breeze through the aspens nearby, the plash and drip of oars on the river below, and now and then the melancholy *tink-tunk* of a sheep bell from one of the flock on the lawn. The flock was a fancy of Hugh's. He swore that nothing was better for a lawn than a few sheep grazing on it, and every summer five or six fat and sleepy ewes were turned out on the grass to serve this purpose and to add a pleasantly pastoral note to the view.

My first warning of something amiss came from the sheep – from the sudden sound of their bells clanging wildly and then baa-ing which suggested an assault by a whole pack of wolves. I heard Hugh say 'Damn!' loudly and angrily, and I opened my eyes to see something more incongruous than wolves. It was a large black poodle in the full glory of a clownish haircut, a bright-red collar, and an ecstasy of high spirits as he chased the frightened sheep around the lawn. It was clear the poodle had no intention of hurting them – he probably found them the most wonderful playmates imaginable – but it was just as clear that the panicky ewes didn't understand this, and would very likely end up in the river before the fun was over.

In the bare second it took me to see all this, Hugh had already leaped the low terrace wall and was among the sheep, herding them away from the water's edge, and shouting commands at the dog who had different ideas.

'Down, boy!' he yelled. 'Down!' And then as he would to one of his own hounds, he sternly commanded, 'Heel!'

He would have done better, I thought, to have picked up a stick or stone and made a threatening gesture, since the poodle paid no attention whatever to Hugh's words. Instead, continuing to bark happily, the poodle made for the sheep again, this time with Hugh in futile pursuit. An instant later the dog was frozen into immobility by a voice from among the aspens near the edge of the lawn.

'*Assieds!*' the voice called breathlessly. '*Assieds-toi!*'

Then the man appeared, a small, dapper figure trotting across the grass. Hugh stood waiting, his face darkening as we watched.

Elizabeth squeezed my arm. 'Let's get down there,' she whispered. 'Hugh doesn't like being made a fool of.'

We got there in time to hear Hugh open his big guns. 'Any man,' he was saying, 'who doesn't know how to train an animal to its place shouldn't own one.'

The man's face was all polite attention. It was a good face, thin and intelligent, and webbed with tiny lines at the corners of the eyes. There was also something behind those eyes that couldn't quite be masked. A gentle mockery. A glint of wry perception turned on the world like a camera lens. It was nothing anyone like Hugh would have noticed, but it was there all the same, and I found myself warming to it on the spot. There was also something tantalizingly familiar about the newcomer's face, his high forehead, and his thinning grey hair, but as much as I dug into my memory during Hugh's long and solemn lecture I couldn't come up with an answer. The lecture ended with a few remarks on the best methods of dog training, and by then it was clear that Hugh was working himself into a mood of forgiveness.

'As long as there's no harm done – ' he said.

The man nodded soberly. 'Still, to get off on the wrong foot with one's new neighbours – '

Hugh looked startled. 'Neighbours?' he said almost rudely. 'You mean that you live around here?'

The man waved toward the aspens. 'On the other side of those woods.'

'The *Dane* house?' The Dane house was almost as sacred to

Hugh as Hilltop, and he had once explained to me that if he were ever offered a chance to buy the place he would snap it up. His tone now was not so much wounded as incredulous. 'I don't believe it!' he exclaimed.

'Oh, yes,' the man assured him, 'the Dane house. I performed there at a party many years ago, and always hoped that some day I might own it.'

It was the word *performed* which gave me my clue – that and the accent barely perceptible under the precise English. He had been born and raised in Marseilles – that would explain the accent – and long before my time he had already become a legend.

'You're Raymond, aren't you?' I said. 'Charles Raymond.'

'I prefer Raymond alone.' He smiled in deprecation of his own small vanity. 'And I am flattered that you recognize me.'

I don't believe he really was. Raymond the Magician, Raymond the Great, would, if anything, expect to be recognized wherever he went. As the master of sleight of hand who had paled Thurston's star, as the escape artist who had almost outshone Houdini, Raymond would not be inclined to underestimate himself.

He had started with the standard box of tricks which makes up the repertoire of most professional magicians; he had gone far beyond that to those feats of escape which, I suppose, are known to us all by now. The lead casket sealed under a foot of lake ice, the welded-steel straitjackets, the vaults of the Bank of England, the exquisite suicide knot which nooses throat and doubles legs together so that the motion of a leg draws the noose tighter around the throat – all these Raymond had known and escaped from. And then at the pinnacle of fame he had dropped from sight and his name had become relegated to the past.

When I asked him why, he shrugged.

'A man works for money or for the love of his work. If he has all the wealth he needs and has no more love for his work, why go on?'

'But to give up a great career – ' I protested.

'It was enough to know that the house was waiting here.'

'You mean,' Elizabeth said, 'that you never intended to live any place but here?'

'Never – not once in all these years.' He laid a finger along his

nose and winked broadly at us. 'Of course, I made no secret of
this to the Dane estate, and when the time came to sell I was the
first and only one approached.'

'You don't give up an idea easily,' Hugh said in an edged voice.

Raymond laughed. 'Idea? It became an obsession really. Over
the years I travelled to many parts of the world, but no matter
how fine the place, I knew it could not be as fine as that house on
the edge of the woods there, with the river at its feet and the hills
beyond. Some day, I would tell myself, when my travels are done
I will come here, and, like Candide, cultivate my garden.'

He ran his hand abstractedly over the poodle's head and looked
around with an air of great satisfaction. 'And now,' he said, 'here
I am.'

Here he was, indeed, and it quickly became clear that his arrival
was working a change on Hilltop. Or, since Hilltop was so completely a reflection of Hugh, it was clear that a change was being
worked on Hugh. He became irritable and restless, and more
aggressively sure of himself than ever. The warmth and good
nature were still there – they were as much part of him as his
arrogance – but he now had to work a little harder at them. He
reminded me of a man who is bothered by a speck in the eye, but
can't find it, and must get along with it as best he can.

Raymond, of course, was the speck, and I got the impression
at times that he rather enjoyed the role. It would have been easy
enough for him to stay close to his own house and cultivate his
garden, or paste up his album, or whatever retired performers do,
but he evidently found that impossible. He had a way of drifting
over to Hilltop at odd times, just as Hugh was led to find his way
to the Dane house and spend long and troublesome sessions
there.

Both of them must have known that they were so badly suited
to each other that the easy and logical solution would have been
to stay apart. But they had the affinity of negative and positive
forces, and when they were in a room together the crackling of
the antagonistic current between them was so strong you could
almost see it in the air.

Any subject became a point of contention for them, and they

would duel over it bitterly: Hugh armoured and weaponed by his massive assurance, Raymond flicking away with a rapier, trying to find a chink in the armour. I think that what annoyed Raymond most was the discovery that there was no chink in the armour. As someone with an obvious passion for searching out all sides to all questions and for going deep into motives and causes, he was continually being outraged by Hugh's single-minded way of laying down the law.

He didn't hesitate to let Hugh know that. 'You are positively medieval,' he said. 'And of all things men should have learned since that time, the biggest is that there are no easy answers, no solutions one can give with a snap of the fingers. I can only hope for you that some day you may be faced with the perfect dilemma, the unanswerable question. You would find that a revelation. You would learn more in that minute than you dreamed possible.'

And Hugh did not make matters any better when he coldly answered: 'And *I* say, that for any man with a brain and the courage to use it there is no such thing as a perfect dilemma.'

It may be that this was the sort of episode that led to the trouble that followed, or it may be that Raymond acted out of the most innocent and aesthetic motives possible. But, whatever the motives, the results were inevitable and dangerous.

They grew from the project Raymond outlined for us in great detail one afternoon. Now that he was living in the Dane house he had discovered that it was too big, too overwhelming. 'Like a museum,' he explained. 'I find myself wandering through it like a lost soul through endless galleries.'

The grounds also needed landscaping. The ancient trees were handsome, but, as Raymond put it, there were just too many of them. 'Literally,' he said, 'I cannot see the river for the trees, and I am one devoted to the sight of running water.'

Altogether there would be drastic changes. Two wings of the house would come down, the trees would be cleared away to make a broad aisle to the water, the whole place would be enlivened. It would no longer be a museum, but the perfect home he had envisioned over the years.

At the start of this recitative Hugh was slouched comfortably in his chair. Then as Raymond drew the vivid picture of what was to be, Hugh sat up straighter and straighter until he was as rigid as a trooper in the saddle. His lips compressed. His face became blood-red. His hands clenched and unclenched in a slow deadly rhythm. Only a miracle was restraining him from an open outburst; it was not the kind of miracle to last. I saw from Elizabeth's expression that she understood this, too, but was as helpless as I to do anything about it. And when Raymond, after painting the last glowing strokes of his description, said complacently, 'Well, now, what do you think?' there was no holding Hugh.

He leaned forward with deliberation and said, 'Do you really want to know what I think?'

'Now, Hugh,' Elizabeth said in alarm. 'Please, Hugh – '

He brushed that aside.

'Do you really want to know?' he demanded of Raymond.

Raymond frowned. 'Of course.'

'Then I'll tell you,' Hugh said. He took a deep breath. 'I think that nobody but a damned iconoclast could even conceive the atrocity you're proposing. I think you're one of those people who take pleasure in smashing apart anything that's stamped with tradition or stability. You'd kick the props from under the whole world if you could!'

'I beg your pardon,' Raymond said. He was very pale and angry. 'But I think you are confusing change with destruction. Surely, you must comprehend that I do not intend to destroy anything, but only wish to make some necessary changes.'

'Necessary?' Hugh gibed. 'Rooting up a fine stand of trees that's been there for centuries? Ripping apart a house that's as solid as a rock? *I* call it wanton destruction.'

'I'm afraid I do not understand. To refresh a scene, to reshape it – '

'I have no intention of arguing,' Hugh cut in. 'I'm telling you straight out that you don't have the right to tamper with that property!'

They were on their feet now, facing each other truculently, and the only thing that kept me from being really frightened was the conviction that Hugh would not become violent, and that Raymond was far too level-headed to lose his temper. Then the threatening moment was magically past. Raymond's lips suddenly quirked in amusement, and he studied Hugh with courteous interest.

'I see,' he said. 'I was quite stupid not to have understood at once. This property, which, I remarked, was a little too much like a museum, is to remain that way, and I am to be its custodian. A caretaker of the past, one might say, a curator of its relics.'

He shook his head smilingly. 'But I am afraid I am not quite suited to that role. I lift my hat to the past, it is true, but I prefer to court the present. For that reason I will go ahead with my plans, and hope they do not make an obstacle to our friendship.'

I remember thinking, when I left next day for the city and a long, hot week at my desk, that Raymond had carried off the affair very nicely, and that, thank God, it had gone no further than it did. So I was completely unprepared for Elizabeth's call at the end of the week.

It was awful, she said. It was the business of Hugh and Raymond and the Dane house, but worse than ever. She was counting on my coming down to Hilltop the next day; there couldn't be any question about that. She had planned a way of clearing up the whole thing, but I simply had to be there to back her up. After all, I was one of the few people Hugh would listen to, and she was depending on me.

'Depending on me for what?' I said. I didn't like the sound of it. 'And as for Hugh listening to me, Elizabeth, isn't that stretching it a good deal? I can't see him wanting my advice on his personal affairs.'

'If you're going to be touchy about it – '

'I'm *not* touchy about it,' I retorted. 'I just don't like getting mixed up in this thing. Hugh's quite capable of taking care of himself.'

'Maybe too capable.'

'And what does that mean?'

'Oh, I can't explain now,' she wailed. 'I'll tell you everything tomorrow. And, darling, if you have any brotherly feelings you'll be here on the morning train. Believe me, it's serious.'

I arrived on the morning train in a bad state. My imagination is one of the overactive kind that can build a cosmic disaster out of very little material, and by the time I arrived at the house I was prepared for almost anything.

But, on the surface, at least, all was serene. Hugh greeted me warmly, Elizabeth was her cheerful self, and we had an amiable lunch and a long talk which never came near the subject of Raymond or the Dane house. I said nothing about Elizabeth's phone call, but thought of it with a steadily growing sense of outrage until I was alone with her.

'Now,' I said, 'I'd like an explanation of all this mystery. The Lord knows what I expected to find out here, but it certainly wasn't anything I've seen so far. And I'd like some accounting for the bad time you've given me since that call.'

'All right,' she said grimly, 'and that's what you'll get. Come along.'

She led the way on a long walk through the gardens and past the stables and outbuildings. Near the private road which lay beyond the last grove of trees she suddenly said, 'When the car drove you up to the house didn't you notice anything strange about this road?'

'No, I didn't.'

'I suppose not. The driveway to the house turns off too far away from here. But now you'll have a chance to see for yourself.'

I did see for myself. A chair was set squarely in the middle of the road and on the chair sat a stout man placidly reading a magazine. I recognized the man at once: he was one of Hugh's stable hands, and he had the patient look of someone who has been sitting for a long time and expects to sit a good deal longer. It took me only a second to realize what he was there for, but Elizabeth wasn't leaving anything to my deductive powers. When we walked over to him, the man stood up and grinned at us.

'William,' Elizabeth said, 'would you mind telling my brother what instructions Mr Lozier gave you?'

'Sure,' the man said cheerfully. 'Mr Lozier told us there was always supposed to be one of us sitting right here, and any truck we saw that might be carrying construction stuff or suchlike for the Dane house was to be stopped and turned back. All we had to do was tell them it's private property and they were trespassing.

If they laid a finger on us we just call in the police. That's the whole thing.'

'Have you turned back any trucks?' Elizabeth asked for my benefit.

The man looked surprised. 'Why, you know that, Mrs Lozier,' he said. 'There was a couple of them the first day we were out here, and that was all. There wasn't any fuss either,' he explained to me. 'None of those drivers wants to monkey with trepass.'

When we were away from the road again I clapped my hand to my forehead. 'It's incredible!' I said. 'Hugh must know he can't get away with this. That road is the only one to the Dane place, and it's been in public use so long that it isn't even a private thoroughfare any more!'

Elizabeth nodded. 'And that's exactly what Raymond told Hugh a few days back. He came over here in a fury, and they had quite an argument about it. And when Raymond said something about hauling Hugh off to court, Hugh answered that he'd be glad to spend the rest of his life in litigation over this business. But that wasn't the worst of it. The last thing Raymond said was that Hugh ought to know that force only invites force, and ever since then I've been expecting a war to break out here any minute. Don't you see? That man blocking the road is a constant provocation, and it scares me.'

I could understand that. And the more I considered the matter, the more dangerous it looked.

'But I have a plan,' Elizabeth said eagerly, 'and that's why I wanted you here. I'm having a dinner party tonight, a very small informal dinner party. It's to be a sort of peace conference. You'll be there, and Dr Wynant – Hugh likes you both a great deal – and,' she hesitated, 'Raymond.'

'No!' I said. 'You mean he's actually coming?'

'I went over to see him yesterday and we had a long talk. I explained everything to him – about neighbours being able to sit down and come to an understanding, and about brotherly love and – oh, it must have sounded dreadfully inspirational and sticky, but it worked. He said he would be there.'

I had a foreboding. 'Does Hugh know about this?'

'About the dinner? Yes.'

'I mean, about Raymond's being here.'

'No, he doesn't.' And then when she saw me looking hard at her, she burst out defiantly with, 'Well, *something* had to be done, and I did it, that's all! Isn't it better than just sitting and waiting for God knows what?'

Until we were all seated around the dining-room table that evening I might have conceded the point. Hugh had been visibly shocked by Raymond's arrival, but then, apart from a sidelong glance at Elizabeth which had volumes written in it, he managed to conceal his feelings well enough. He had made the introductions gracefully, kept up his end of the conversation, and, all in all, did a creditable job of playing host.

Ironically, it was the presence of Dr Wynant which made even this much of a triumph possible for Elizabeth, and which then turned it into disaster. The doctor was an eminent surgeon, stocky and grey-haired, with an abrupt, positive way about him. Despite his own position in the world he seemed pleased as a schoolboy to meet Raymond, and in no time at all they were as thick as thieves.

It was when Hugh discovered during dinner that nearly all attention was fixed on Raymond and very little on himself that the mantle of good host started to slip, and the fatal flaws in Elizabeth's plan showed through. There are people who enjoy entertaining lions and who take pleasure in reflected glory, but Hugh was not one of them. Besides, he regarded the doctor as one of his closest friends, and I have noticed that it is the most assured of men who can be the most jealous of their friendships. And when a prized friendship is being impinged on by the man one loathes more than anything else in the world – ! All in all, by simply imagining myself in Hugh's place and looking across the table at Raymond who was gaily and unconcernedly holding forth, I was prepared for the worst.

The opportunity for it came to Hugh when Raymond was deep in a discussion of the devices used in effecting escapes. They were innumerable, he said. Almost anything one could seize on would serve as such a device. A wire, a scrap of metal, even a bit of paper – at one time or another he had used them all.

'But of them all,' he said with a sudden solemnity, 'there is only one I would stake my life on. Strange, it is one you cannot see, cannot hold in your hand – in fact, for many people it does not even exist. Yet it is the one I have used most often and which has never failed me.'

The doctor leaned forward, his eyes bright with interest. 'And it is – ?'

'It is a knowledge of people, my friend. Or, as it may be put, a knowledge of human nature. To me it is as vital an instrument as the scalpel is to you.'

'Oh?' said Hugh, and his voice was so sharp that all eyes were instantly turned on him. 'You make sleight of hand sound like a department of psychology.'

'Perhaps,' Raymond said, and I saw he was watching Hugh now, gauging him. 'You see there is no great mystery in the matter. My profession – my art, as I like to think of it – is no more than the art of misdirection, and I am but one of its many practitioners.'

'I wouldn't say there were many escape artists around nowadays,' the doctor remarked.

'True,' Raymond said, 'but you will observe I referred to the art of misdirection. The escape artist, the master of legerdemain, these are a handful who practise the most exotic form of that art. But what of those who engage in the work of politics, of advertising, of salesmanship?' He laid his finger along his nose in the familiar gesture, and winked. 'I am afraid they have all made my art their business.'

The doctor smiled. 'Since you haven't dragged medicine into it I'm willing to go along with you,' he said. 'But what I want to know is, exactly how does this knowledge of human nature work in your profession?'

'In this way,' Raymond said. 'One must judge a person carefully. Then, if he finds in that person certain weaknesses, he can state a false premise and it will be accepted without question. Once the false premise is swallowed, the rest is easy. The victim will then see only what the magician wants him to see, or will give his vote to that politician, or will buy merchandise because of that advertising.' He shrugged. 'And that is all there is to it.'

'Is it?' Hugh said. 'But what happens when you're with people who have some intelligence and won't swallow your false premise? How do you do your tricks then? Or do you keep them on the same level as selling beads to the savages?'

'Now that's uncalled for, Hugh,' the doctor said. 'The man's expressing his ideas. No reason to make an issue of them.'

'Maybe there is,' Hugh said, his eyes fixed on Raymond. 'I have found he's full of interesting ideas. I was wondering how far he'd want to go in backing them up.'

Raymond touched the napkin to his lips with a precise little flick, and then laid it carefully on the table before him. 'In short,' he said, addressing himself to Hugh, 'you want a small demonstration of my art.'

'It depends,' Hugh said. 'I don't want any trick cigarette cases or rabbits out of hats or any damn nonsense like that. I'd like to see something good.'

'Something good,' echoed Raymond reflectively. He looked around the room, studied it, and then turned to Hugh, pointing toward the huge oak door which was closed between the dining room and the living room, where we had gathered before dinner.

'That door is not locked, is it?'

'No,' Hugh said, 'it isn't. It hasn't been locked for years.'

'But there is a key to it?'

Hugh pulled out his key chain, and with an effort detached a heavy, old-fashioned key. 'Yes, it's the same one we use for the butler's pantry.' He was becoming interested despite himself.

'Good. No, do not give it to me. Give it to the doctor. You have faith in the doctor's honour, I am sure?'

'Yes,' said Hugh drily, 'I have.'

'Very well. Now, Doctor, will you please go to that door and lock it.'

The doctor marched to the door, with his firm, decisive tread, thrust the key into the lock, and turned it. The click of the bolt snapping into place was loud in the silence of the room. The doctor returned to the table holding the key, but Raymond motioned it away. 'It must not leave your hand or everything is lost,' he warned.

'Now,' Raymond said, 'for the finale I approach the door, I flick my handkerchief at it – ' the handkerchief barely brushed the keyhole ' – and presto, the door is unlocked!'

The doctor went to it. He seized the doorknob, twisted it dubiously, and then watched with genuine astonishment as the door swung silently open.

'Well, I'll be damned,' he said.

'Somehow,' Elizabeth laughed, 'a false premise went down easy as an oyster.'

Only Hugh reflected a sense of personal outrage. 'All right,' he demanded, 'how was it done? How did you work it?'

'I?' Raymond said reproachfully, and smiled at all of us with obvious enjoyment. 'It was you who did it all. I used only my little knowledge of human nature to help you along the way.'

I said, 'I can guess part of it. That door was set in advance, and when the doctor thought he was locking it, he wasn't. He was really unlocking it. Isn't that the answer?'

Raymond nodded. 'Very much the answer. The door *was* locked in advance. I made sure of that, because with a little forethought I suspected there would be such a challenge during the evening, and this was the simplest way of preparing for it. I merely made certain that I was the last one to enter this room, and when I did I used this.' He held up his hand so that we could see the sliver of metal in it. 'An ordinary skeleton key, of course, but sufficient for an old and primitive lock.'

For a moment Raymond looked grave, then he continued brightly, 'It was our host himself who stated the false premise when he said the door was unlocked. He was a man so sure of himself that he would not think to test anything so obvious. The doctor is also a man who is sure, and he fell into the same trap. It is, as you now see, a little dangerous always to be so sure.'

'I'll go along with that,' the doctor said ruefully, 'even though it's heresy to admit it in my line of work.' He playfully tossed the key he had been holding across the table to Hugh who let it fall in front of him and made no gesture toward it. 'Well, Hugh, like it or not, you must admit the man has proved his point.'

'Do I?' said Hugh softly. He sat there smiling a little now, and it was easy to see he was turning some thought over and over in his head.

'Oh, come on, man,' the doctor said with some impatience. 'You were taken in as much as we were. You know that.'

'Of course you were, darling,' Elizabeth agreed.

I think that she suddenly saw her opportunity to turn the proceedings into the peace conference she had aimed at, but I could have told her she was choosing her time badly. There was a look in Hugh's eye I didn't like – a veiled look which wasn't natural to him. Ordinarily, when he was really angered, he would blow up a violent storm, and once the thunder and lightning had passed he would be honestly apologetic. But this present mood of his was different. There was a slumbrous quality in it which alarmed me.

He hooked one arm over the back of his chair and rested the other on the table, sitting halfway around to fix his eyes on Raymond. 'I seem to be a minority of one,' he remarked, 'but I'm sorry to say I found your little trick disappointing. Not that it wasn't cleverly done – I'll grant that, all right – but because it wasn't any more than you'd expect from a competent locksmith.'

'Now there's a large helping of sour grapes,' the doctor jeered.

Hugh shook his head. 'No, I'm simply saying that where there's a lock on a door and the key to it in your hand, it's no great trick to open it. Considering our friend's reputation, I thought we'd see more from him than that.'

Raymond grimaced. 'Since I had hoped to entertain,' he said, 'I must apologize for disappointing.'

'Oh, as far as entertainment goes I have no complaints. But for a real test – '

'A real test?'

'Yes, something a little different. Let's say, a door without any locks or keys to tamper with. A closed door which can be opened with a fingertip, but which is nevertheless impossible to open. How does that sound to you?'

Raymond narrowed his eyes thoughtfully, as if he were considering the picture being presented to him. 'It sounds most interesting,' he said at last. 'Tell me more about it.'

'No,' Hugh said, and from the sudden eagerness in his voice I felt that this was the exact moment he had been looking for. 'I'll do better than that. I'll *show* it to you.'

He stood up brusquely and the rest of us followed suit – except Elizabeth, who remained in her seat. When I asked her if she wanted to come along, she only shook her head and sat there watching us hopelessly as we left the room.

We were bound for the cellars, I realized, when Hugh picked up a flashlight along the way, but for a part of the cellars I had never seen before. On a few occasions I had gone downstairs to help select a bottle of wine from the racks there, but now we walked past the wine vault and into a long, dimly lit chamber behind it. Our feet scraped loudly on the rough stone, the walls around us showed the stains of seepage, and warm as the night was outside, I could feel the chill of dampness turning my chest to gooseflesh. When the doctor shuddered and said hollowly, 'These are the very tombs of Atlantis,' I knew I wasn't alone in my feeling, and felt some relief at that.

We stopped at the very end of the chamber, before what I can best describe as a stone closet built from floor to ceiling in the farthest angle of the walls. It was about four feet wide and not quite twice that in length, and its open doorway showed impenetrable blackness inside. Hugh reached into the blackness and pulled a heavy door into place.

'That's it,' he said abruptly. 'Plain solid wood, four inches thick, fitted flush into the frame so that it's almost airtight. It's a beautiful piece of carpentry, too, the kind they practised two hundred years ago. And no locks or bolts. Just a ring set into each side to use as a handle.' He pushed the door gently and it swung open noiselessly at his touch. 'See that? The whole thing is balanced so perfectly on the hinges that it moves like a feather.'

'But what is it for?' I asked. 'It must have been made for a reason.'

Hugh laughed shortly. 'It was. Back in the bad old days, when a servant committed a crime – and I don't suppose it had to be more of a crime than talking back to one of the ancient Loziers – he was put in here to repent. And since the air inside was good for only a few hours at the most, he either repented damn soon or not at all.'

'And that door?' the doctor said cautiously. 'That impressive door of yours which opens at a touch to provide all the air needed – what prevented the servant from opening it?'

'Look,' Hugh said. He flashed his light inside the cell and we

crowded behind him to peer in. The circle of light reached across
the cell to its far wall and picked out a short, heavy chain hanging
a little above head level with a U-shaped collar dangling from its
bottom link.

'I see,' Raymond said, and they were the first words I had heard
him speak since we had left the dining room. 'It is truly ingenious.
The man stands with his back against the wall, facing the door.
The collar is placed around his neck, and then – since it is clearly
not made for a lock – it is clamped there, hammered around his
neck. The door is closed, and the man spends the next few hours
like someone on an invisible rack, reaching out with his feet to
catch the ring on the door which is just out of reach. If he is
lucky he may not strangle himself in his iron collar, but may live
until someone chooses to open the door for him.'

'My God,' the doctor said. 'You make me feel as if I were
living through it.'

Raymond smiled faintly. 'I have lived through many such
experiences, and, believe me, the reality is always a little worse
than the worst imaginings. There is always the ultimate moment
of terror, of panic, when the heart pounds so madly you think it
will burst through your ribs, and the cold sweat soaks clear
through you in the space of one breath. That is when you must
take yourself in hand, must dispel all weakness, and remember
all the lessons you have ever learned. If not – !' He whisked the
edge of his hand across his lean throat. 'Unfortunately for the
usual victim of such a device,' he concluded sadly, 'since he lacks
the essential courage and knowledge to help himself, he succumbs.'

'But you wouldn't,' Hugh said.

'I have no reason to think so.'

'You mean,' and the eagerness was creeping back into Hugh's
voice, stronger than ever, 'that under the very same conditions as
someone chained in there two hundred years ago you could get
this door open?'

The challenging note was too strong to be brushed aside
lightly. Raymond stood silent for a long minute, face strained
with concentration, before he answered.

'Yes,' he said. 'It would not be easy – the problem is made
formidable by its very simplicity – but it could be solved.'

'How long do you think it would take you?'

'An hour at the most.'

Hugh had come a long way around to get to this point. He asked the question slowly, savouring it. 'Would you want to bet on that?'

'Now, wait a minute,' the doctor said. 'I don't like any part of this.'

'And I vote we adjourn for a drink,' I put in. 'Fun's fun, but we'll all wind up with pneumonia, playing games down here.'

Neither Hugh nor Raymond appeared to hear a word of this. They stood staring at each other – Hugh waiting on pins and needles, Raymond deliberating – until Raymond said, 'What is this bet you offer?'

'This. If you lose, you get out of the Dane house inside of a month, and sell it to me.'

'And if I win?'

It was not easy for Hugh to say it, but he finally got it out. 'Then I'll be the one to get out. And if you don't want to buy Hilltop I'll arrange to sell it to the first comer.'

For anyone who knew Hugh it was so fantastic, so staggering a statement to hear from him, that none of us could find words at first. It was the doctor who recovered most quickly.

'You're not speaking for yourself, Hugh,' he warned. 'You're a married man. Elizabeth's feelings have to be considered.'

'Is it a bet?' Hugh demanded of Raymond. 'Do you want to go through with it?'

'I think before I answer that, there is something to be explained.' Raymond paused, then went on slowly, 'I am afraid I gave the impression – out of pride, perhaps – that when I retired from my work it was because of a boredom, a lack of interest in it. That was not altogether the truth. In reality, I was required to go to a doctor some years ago, the doctor listened to the heart, and suddenly my heart became the most important thing in the world. I tell you this because, while your challenge strikes me as being a most unusual and interesting way of settling differences between neighbours, I must reject it for reasons of health.'

'You were healthy enough a minute ago,' Hugh said in a hard voice.

'Perhaps not as much as you would want to think, my friend.'

'In other words,' Hugh said bitterly, 'there's no accomplice handy, no keys in your pocket to help out, and no way of tricking anyone into seeing what isn't there! So you have to admit you're beaten.'

Raymond stiffened. 'I admit no such thing. All the tools I would need even for such a test as this I have with me. Believe me, they would be enough.'

Hugh laughed aloud, and the sound of it broke into small echoes all down the corridors behind us. It was that sound, I am sure – the living contempt in it rebounding from wall to wall around us – which sent Raymond into the cell.

Hugh wielded the hammer, a short-handled but heavy sledge, which tightened the collar into a circlet around Raymond's neck, hitting with hard even strokes at the iron which was braced against the wall. When he had finished I saw the pale glow of the radium-painted numbers on a watch as Raymond studied it in his pitch darkness.

'It is now eleven,' he said calmly. 'The wager is that by midnight this door must be opened, and it does not matter what means are used. Those are the conditions, and you gentlemen are the witnesses to them.'

Then the door was closed, and the walking began.

Back and forth we walked – the three of us – as if we were being compelled to trace every possible geometric figure on that stony floor, the doctor with his quick, impatient step, and I matching Hugh's long, nervous strides. A foolish, meaningless march, back and forth across our own shadows, each of us marking the time by counting off the passing seconds, and each ashamed to be the first to look at his watch.

For a while there was a counterpoint to this scraping of feet from inside the cell. It was a barely perceptible clinking of chain coming at brief, regular intervals. Then there would be a long silence, followed by a renewal of the sound. When it stopped again I could not restrain myself any longer. I held up my watch toward the dim yellowish light of the bulb overhead and saw with dismay that barely twenty minutes had passed.

After that there was no hesitancy in the others about looking at the time, and, if anything, this made it harder to bear than just wondering. I caught the doctor winding his watch with small, brisk turns, and then a few minutes later he would try to wind it again, and suddenly drop his hand with disgust as he realized he had already done it. Hugh walked with his watch held up near his eyes, as if by concentration on it he could drag that crawling minute hand faster around the dial.

Thirty minutes had passed.

Forty.

Forty-five.

I remember that when I looked at my watch and saw there were less than fifteen minutes to go I wondered if I could last out even that short time. The chill had sunk so deep into me that I ached with it. I was shocked when I saw that Hugh's face was dripping with sweat, and that beads of it gathered and ran off while I watched.

It was while I was looking at him in fascination that it happened. The sound broke through the walls of the cell like a wail of agony heard from far away, and shivered over us as if it were spelling out the words.

'*Doctor*!' it cried. '*The air!*'

It was Raymond's voice, but the thickness of the wall blocking it off turned it into a high, thin sound. What was clearest in it was the note of pure terror, the plea growing out of that terror.

'*Air!*' it screamed, the word bubbling and dissolving into a long-drawn sound which made no sense at all.

And then it was silent.

We leaped for the door together, but Hugh was there first, his back against it, barring the way. In his upraised hand was the hammer which had clinched Raymond's collar.

'Keep back!' he cried. 'Don't come any nearer, I warn you!'

The fury in him, brought home by the menace of the weapon, stopped us in our tracks.

'Hugh,' the doctor pleaded, 'I know what you're thinking, but you can forget that now. The bet's off, and I'm opening the door on my own responsibility. You have my word for that.'

'Do I? But do you remember the terms of the bet, Doctor? This door must be opened within an hour – *and it doesn't matter what means are used*! Do you understand now? He's fooling both of you. He's faking a death scene, so that you'll push open the door and win his bet for him. But it's my bet, not yours, and I have the last word on it!'

I saw from the way he talked, despite the shaking tension in his voice, that he was in perfect command of himself, and it made everything seem that much worse.

'How do you know he's faking?' I demanded. 'The man said he had a heart condition. He said there was always a time in a spot like this when he had to fight panic and could feel the strain of it. What right do you have to gamble with his life?'

'Damn it, don't you see he never mentioned any heart condition until he smelled a bet in the wind? Don't you see he set his trap that way, just as he locked the door behind him when he came in to dinner! But this time nobody will spring it for him – nobody!'

'Listen to me,' the doctor said, and his voice cracked like a whip. 'Do you concede that there's one slim possibility of that man being dead in there, or dying?'

'Yes, it is possible – anything is possible.'

'I'm not trying to split hairs with you! I'm telling you that if that man is in trouble every second counts, and you're stealing that time from him. And if that's the case, by God, I'll sit in the witness chair at your trial and swear you murdered him! Is that what you want?'

Hugh's head sank forward on his chest, but his hand still tightly gripped the hammer. I could hear the breath drawing heavily in his throat, and when he raised his head, his face was grey and haggard. The torment of indecision was written in every pale sweating line of it.

And then I suddenly understood what Raymond had meant that day when he told Hugh about the revelation he might find in the face of a perfect dilemma. It was the revelation of what a man may learn about himself when he is forced to look into his own depths, and Hugh had found it at last.

In that shadowy cellar, while the relentless seconds thundered louder and louder in our ears, we waited to see what he would do.

More about Penguins

Penguin Book News, an attractively illustrated magazine
which appears every month, contains details of all
the new books issued by Penguins as they are published.
Every four months it is supplemented by *Penguins in Print*,
which is a complete list of all books published by
Penguins which are still available. (There are well over
two thousand of these.)

A specimen copy of *Penguin Book News* can be
sent to you on request, and you can become a regular
subscriber at 3s for twelve issues (with the complete lists).
Just write to Dept EP, Penguin Books Ltd,
Harmondsworth, Middlesex, enclosing a cheque or postal
order, and your name will be added to the mailing list.

Some other books published by Penguins are
described on the following pages.

Note: *Penguin Book News* and *Penguins in Print*
are not available in the U.S.A. or Canada

Criminal Conversation

Nicholas Freeling

Van der Valk always got the cases no one else would
touch. The ones that would have been better hushed up.
Rich people, powerful people with friends in high
and low places should be handled with kid gloves.
But Van der Valk wanted to know all their nasty secrets . . .
why a sixteen-year-old girl and her mother were so
involved with a rich society doctor . . . why a drunken
painter who knew too much died so conveniently of
natural causes . . .

Also available

Because of the Cats

Double-Barrel

Gun Before Butter

Love in Amsterdam

Not for sale in the U.S.A.

Ellery Queen

The Player on the Other Side

Ellery Queen meets the mindless man with the motiveless
plan to rid New York society of a conveniently neighbourly
family of very, very rich eccentrics.
And a mindless man is all you need for a perfect crime –
a robot that walks, talks, and does everything you want . . .
except think.

'He has done far more for the detective story than any
other two men put together' – Margery Allingham

'A new Ellery Queen book has always been something to
look forward to for many years now' – Agatha Christie

'They have raised exactitude and efficiency to the degree
of brilliance, and fair play to the point of turpitude.
In their group there is no one to touch them' – Ngaio Marsh

'The Ellery Queens are a phenomenon' – Patrick Quentin

Some more crime fiction in Penguins by Ellery Queen

Not for sale in the U.S.A. or Canada

Stanley Ellin

Dreadful Summit

This is the diary of one night of brainstorm and violence in the life of a teenage boy – a night of initiation into sex and sudden death and heroism.

The lonely, introspective mind of George LaMain had been nourished on Kipling and Dumas. Seeing his father mercilessly flogged by a fashionable sports columnist, the boy simply picks up a gun and goes after the bully. To kill.

That is all. But Stanley Ellin has equipped this little story with the kind of humour, the exactness of detail, and that invading sense of terror that one usually associates with Georges Simenon.

'Powerful, readable piece of violence' – Christopher Pym in the *Spectator*

'The whole book has that nightmarish quality which Mr Ellin manages to combine with his distinctive sort of offbeat realism' – *Sunday Times*

Not for sale in the U.S.A. or Canada

Also by Stanley Ellin

The Eighth Circle

Suspense runs neck-and-neck with insight in this
'new-look' story of a private eye with a blind spot.
To Murray Kirk all policemen are automatically guilty;
when his agency is asked to act for a policeman accused
of bribery, Kirk's motives get too confused for comfort.
In a thriller that moves swiftly through a grey world
of bookmakers, gangsters, grafters, and politicos,
the author of *Dreadful Summit* and *The Key to Nicholas
Street* cracks the cherished image of the 'tough guy'
investigator.